The Wizard by H. Rider Haggard

Sir Henry Rider Haggard, KBE was born on June 22nd, 1856 at Bradenham in Norfolk, England.

After his education he was pushed towards an Army career but failed the entrance exam. Next Haggard was positioned to work for the British Foreign Office but he seems not to have sat that exam. Using family connections, he was sent to Southern Africa by his father in search of a further opportunity of a career.

Haggard spent six years there before a return to England and marriage. He had begun to write and publish some non-fiction in Africa but it was only after studying Law in the hope it might prove to be the proper career his father wanted for him that Haggard began to write fiction, using his African experiences as the basis.

His first fiction was published in 1885 and the following year King Solomon's Mines was published. It was a phenomenal success. His career was set.

Haggard wrote well and wrote often. He managed to sympathise with the local populations even though they were exploited and manipulated by Europeans intent on amassing fortunes in money, people and resources. His writing career covered the great sprint to Empire of several European powers and both reflects and criticizes these events through his well-loved characters including Allan Quatermain and Ayesha.

In his later years Haggard pursued much in the way social reform as well as standing for Parliament and writing a great many letters to The Times.

Henry Rider Haggard died on May 14th, 1925 at the age of 68. His ashes were buried at Ditchingham Church.

Index of Contents

DEDICATION

To the Memory of the Child

Nada Burnham, who "bound all to her" and, while her father cut his way through the hordes of the Ingobo Regiment, perished of the hardships of war at Buluwayo on 19th May, 1896, I dedicate these tales—and more particularly the last, that of a Faith which triumphed over savagery and death.

H. Rider Haggard.
Ditchingham.

CHAPTER I

THE DEPUTATION

Has the age of miracle quite gone by, or is it still possible to the Voice of Faith calling aloud upon the earth to wring from the dumb heavens an audible answer to its prayer? Does the promise uttered by the Master of mankind upon the eve of the end—"Whoso that believeth in Me, the works that I do he shall do also . . . and whatsoever ye shall ask in My name, that will I do;"—still hold good to such as do ask and do believe?

Let those who care to study the history of the Rev. Thomas Owen, and of that strange man who carried on and completed his work, answer this question according to their judgment.

The time was a Sunday afternoon in summer, and the place a church in the Midland counties. It was a beautiful church, ancient and spacious; moreover, it had recently been restored at great cost. Seven or eight hundred people could have found sittings in it, and doubtless they had done so when Busscombe was a large manufacturing town, before the failure of the coal supply and other causes drove away its trade. Now it was much what it had been in the time of the Normans, a little agricultural village with a population of 300 souls. Out of this population, including the choir boys, exactly thirty-nine had elected to attend church on this particular Sunday; and of these, three were fast asleep and four were dozing.

The Rev. Thomas Owen counted them from his seat in the chancel, for another clergyman was preaching; and, as he counted, bitterness and disappointment took hold of him. The preacher was a "Deputation," sent by one of the large missionary societies to arouse the indifferent to a sense of duty towards their unconverted black brethren in Africa, and incidentally to collect cash to be spent in the conversion of the said brethren. The Rev. Thomas Owen himself suggested the visit of the Deputation, and had laboured hard to secure him a good audience. But the beauty of the weather, or terror of the inevitable subscription, prevailed against him. Hence his disappointment.

"Well," he thought, with a sigh, "I have done my best, and I must make it up out of my own pocket."

Then he settled himself to listen to the sermon.

The preacher, a battered-looking individual of between fifty and sixty years of age, was gaunt with recent sickness, patient and unimaginative in aspect. He preached extemporarily, with the aid of notes; and it cannot be said that his discourse was remarkable for interest, at any rate in its beginning. Doubtless the sparse congregation, so prone to slumber, discouraged him; for offering exhortations to empty benches is but weary work. Indeed he was meditating the advisability of bringing his argument to an abrupt conclusion when, chancing to glance round, he became aware that he had at least one sympathetic listener, his host, the Rev. Thomas Owen.

From that moment the sermon improved by degrees, till at length it reached a really high level of excellence. Ceasing from rhetoric, the speaker began to tell of his own experience and sufferings in the Cause amongst savage tribes; for he himself was a missionary of many years standing. He told how once he and a companion had been sent to a nation, who named themselves the Sons of Fire because their god was the lightning, if indeed they could be said to boast any gods other than the Spear and the King. In simple language he narrated his terrible adventures among these savages, the murder of his companion by command of the Council of Wizards, and his own flight for his life; a tale so interesting and vivid that even the bucolic sleepers awakened and listened open-mouthed.

"But this is by the way," he went on; "for my Society does not ask you to subscribe towards the conversion of the Children of Fire. Until that people is conquered—which very likely will not be for generations, seeing that they live in Central Africa, occupying a territory that white men do not desire— no missionary will dare again to visit them."

At this moment something caused him to look a second time at Thomas Owen. He was leaning forward in his place listening eagerly, and a strange light filled the large, dark eyes that shone in the pallor of his delicate, nervous face.

"There is a man who would dare, if he were put to it," thought the Deputation to himself. Then he ended his sermon.

That evening the two men sat at dinner in the rectory. It was a very fine rectory, beautifully furnished; for Owen was a man of taste which he had the means to gratify. Also, although they were alone, the dinner was good—so good that the poor broken-down missionary, sipping his unaccustomed port, a vintage wine, sighed aloud in admiration and involuntary envy.

"What is the matter?" asked Owen.

"Nothing, Mr. Owen;" then, of a sudden thawing into candour, he added: "that is, everything. Heaven forgive me; but I, who enjoy your hospitality, am envious of you. Don't think too hardly of me; I have a large family to support, and if only you knew what a struggle my life is, and has been for the last twenty years, you would not, I am sure. But you have never experienced it, and could not understand. 'The labourer is worthy of his hire.' Well, my hire is under two hundred a year, and eight of us must live—or starve—on it. And I have worked, ay, until my health is broken. A labourer indeed! I am a very hodman, a spiritual Sisyphus. And now I must go back to carry my load and roll my stone again and again among those hopeless savages till I die of it—till I die of it!"

"At least it is a noble life and death!" exclaimed Owen, a sudden fire of enthusiasm burning in his dark eyes.

"Yes, viewed from a distance. Were you asked to leave this living of two thousand a year—I see that is what they put it at in Crockford—with its English comforts and easy work, that you might lead that life and attain that death, then you would think differently. But why should I bore you with such talk? Thank Heaven that your lines are cast in pleasant places. Yes, please, I will take one more glass; it does me good."

"Tell me some more about that tribe you were speaking of in your sermon, the 'Sons of Fire' I think you called them," said Owen, as he passed him the decanter.

So, with an eloquence induced by the generous wine and a quickened imagination, the Deputation told him—told him many strange things and terrible. For this people was an awful people: vigorous in mind and body, and warriors from generation to generation, but superstition-ridden and cruel. They lived in the far interior, some months' journey by boat and ox-waggon from the coast, and of white men and their ways they knew but little.

"How many of them are there?" asked Owen.

"Who can say?" he answered. "Nearly half-a-million, perhaps; at least they pretend that they can put sixty thousand men under arms."

"And did they treat you badly when you first visited them?"

"Not at first. They received us civilly enough; and on a given day we were requested to explain to the king and the Council of Wizards the religion which we came to teach. All that day we explained and all the next—or rather my friend did, for I knew very little of the language—and they listened with great interest. At last the chief of the wizards and the first prophet to the king rose to question us. He was named Hokosa, a tall, thin man, with a spiritual face and terrible calm eyes.

"'You speak well, son of a White Man,' he said, 'but let us pass from words to deeds. You tell us that this God of yours, whom you desire that we should take as our God, so that you may become His chief prophets in the land, was a wizard such as we are, though grater than we are; for not only did He know the past and the future as we do, but also He could cure those who were smitten with hopeless sickness, and raise those who were dead, which we cannot do. You tell us, moreover, that by faith those who believe on Him can do works as great as He did, and that you do believe on Him. Therefore we will put you to the proof. Ho! there, lead forth that evil one.'

"As he spoke a man was placed before us, one who had been convicted of witchcraft or some other crime.

"'Kill him!' said Hokosa.

"There was a faint cry, a scuffle, a flashing of spears, and the man lay still before us.

"'Now, followers of the new God,' said Hokosa, 'raise him from the dead as your Master did!'

"In vain did we offer explanations.

"'Peace!' said Hokosa at length, 'your words weary us. Look now, either you have preached to us a false god and are liars, or you are traitors to the King you preach, since, lacking faith in Him, you cannot do such works as He gives power to do to those who have faith in Him. Out of your own mouths are you judged, White Men. Choose which horn of the bull you will, you hang to one of them, and it shall pierce you. This is the sentence of the king, I speak it who am the king's mouth: That you, White Man, who have spoken to us and cheated us these two weary days, be put to death, and that you, his companion who have been silent, be driven from the land.'

"I can hardly bear to tell the rest of it, Mr. Owen. They gave my poor friend ten minutes to 'talk to his Spirit,' then they speared him before my face. After it was over, Hokosa spoke to me, saying:—

"'Go back, White Man, to those who sent you, and tell them the words of the Sons of Fire: That they have listened to the message of peace, and though they are a people of warriors, yet they thank them for that message, for in itself it sounds good and beautiful in their ears, if it be true. Tell them that having proved you liars, they dealt with you as all honest men seek that liars should be dealt with. Tell them that they desire to hear more of this matter, and if one can be sent to them who has no false tongue; who in all things fulfills the promises of his lips, that they will hearken to him and treat him well, but that for such as you they keep a spear.'"

"And who went after you got back?" asked Owen, who was listening with the deepest interest.

"Who went? Do you suppose that there are many mad clergymen in Africa, Mr. Owen? Nobody went."

"And yet," said Owen, speaking more to himself than to his guest, "the man Hokosa was right, and the Christian who of a truth believes the promises of our religion should trust to them and go."

"Then perhaps you would like to undertake the mission, Mr. Owen," said the Deputation briskly; for the reflection stung him, unintentional as it was.

Owen started.

"That is a new idea," he said. "And now perhaps you wish to go to bed; it is past eleven o'clock."

CHAPTER II

THOMAS OWEN

Thomas Owen went to his room, but not to bed. Taking a Bible from the table, he consulted reference after reference.

"The promise is clear," he said aloud presently, as he shut the book; "clear and often repeated. There is no escape from it, and no possibility of a double meaning. If it is not true, then it would seem that nothing is true, and that every Christian in the world is tricked and deluded. But if it is true, why do we never hear of miracles? The answer is easy: Because we have not faith enough to work them. The Apostles worked miracles; for they had seen, therefore their faith was perfect. Since their day nobody's faith has been quite perfect; at least I think not. The physical part of our nature prevents it. Or perhaps the miracles still happen, but they are spiritual miracles."

Then he sat down by the open window, and gazing at the dreamy beauty of the summer night, he thought, for his soul was troubled. Once before it had been troubled thus; that was nine years ago, for now he was but little over thirty. Then a call had come to him, a voice had seemed to speak to his ears bidding him to lay down great possessions to follow whither Heaven should lead him. Thomas Owen had obeyed the voice; though, owing to circumstances which need not be detailed, to do so he was obliged to renounce his succession to a very large estate, and to content himself with a younger son's portion of thirty thousand pounds and the reversion to the living which he had now held for some five years.

Then and there, with singular unanimity and despatch, his relations came to the conclusion that he was mad. To this hour, indeed, those who stand in his place and enjoy the wealth and position that were his by right, speak of him as "poor Thomas," and mark their disapprobation of his peculiar conduct by refusing with an unvarying steadiness to subscribe even a single shilling to a missionary society. How "poor Thomas" speaks of them in the place where he is we may wonder, but as yet we cannot know— probably with the gentle love and charity that marked his every action upon earth. But this is by the way.

He had entered the Church, but what had he done in its shadow? This was the question which Owen asked himself as he sat that night by the open window, arraigning his past before the judgment-seat of conscience. For three years he had worked hard somewhere in the slums; then this living had fallen to him. He had taken it, and from that day forward his record was very much of a blank. The parish was small and well ordered; there was little to do in it, and the Salvation Army had seized upon and reclaimed two of the three confirmed drunkards it could boast.

His guest's saying echoed in his brain like the catch of a tune—"that you might lead that life and attain that death." Supposing that he were bidden so to do now, this very night, would he indeed "think differently"? He had become a priest to serve his Maker. How would it be were that Maker to command that he should serve Him in this extreme and heroic fashion? Would he flinch from the steel, or would he meet it as the martyrs met it of old?

Physically he was little suited to such an enterprise, for in appearance he was slight and pale, and in constitution delicate. Also, there was another reason against the thing. High Church and somewhat ascetic in his principles, in the beginning he had admired celibacy, and in secret dedicated himself to that state. But at heart Thomas was very much a man, and of late he had come to see that which is against nature is presumably not right, though fanatics may not hesitate to pronounce it wrong. Possibly this conversion to more genial views of life was quickened by the presence in the neighbourhood of a young lady whom he chanced to admire; at least it is certain that the mere thought of seeing her no more for ever smote him like a sword of sudden pain.

That very night—or so it seemed to him, and so he believed—the Angel of the Lord stood before him as he was wont to stand before the men of old, and spoke a summons in his ear. How or in what seeming that summons came Thomas Owen never told, and we need not inquire. At the least he heard it, and, like the Apostles, he arose and girded his loins to obey. For now, in the hour of trial, it proved that this man's faith partook of the nature of their faith. It was utter and virgin; it was not clogged with nineteenth-century qualifications; it had never dallied with strange doctrines, or kissed the feet of pinchbeck substitutes for God. In his heart he believed that the Almighty, without intermediary, but face to face, had bidden him to go forth into the wilderness there to perish. So he bowed his head and went.

On the following morning at breakfast Owen had some talk with his friend the Deputation.

"You asked me last night," he said quietly, "whether I would undertake a mission to that people of whom you were telling me—the Sons of Fire. Well, I have been thinking it over, and come to the conclusion that I will do so—"

At this point the Deputation, concluding that his host must be mad, moved quietly but decidedly towards the door.

"Wait a moment," went on Owen, in a matter-of-fact voice, "the dog-cart will not be round for another three-quarters of an hour. Tell me, if it were offered to you, and on investigation you proved suitable, would you care to take over this living?"

"Would I care to take over this living?" gasped the astonished Deputation. "Would I care to walk down that garden and find myself in Heaven? But why are you making fun of me?"

"I am not making fun of you. If I go to Africa I must give up the living, of which I own the advowson, and it occurred to me that it might suit you—that is all. You have done your share; your health is broken, and you have many dependent upon you. It seems right, therefore, that you should rest, and that I should work. If I do no good yonder, at the least you and yours will be a little benefited."

That same day Owen chanced to meet the lady who has been spoken of as having caught his heart. He had meant to go away without seeing her, but fortune brought them together. Hitherto, whilst in reality leading him on, she had seemed to keep him at a distance, with the result that he did not know that it was her fixed intention to marry him. To her, with some hesitation, he told his plans. Surprised and frightened into candour, the lady reasoned with him warmly, and when reason failed to move him she did more. By some subtle movement, with some sudden word, she lifted the veil of her reserve and suffered him to see her heart. "If you will not stay for aught else," said her troubled eyes, "then, love, stay for me."

For a moment he was shaken. Then he answered the look straight out, as was his nature.

"I never guessed," he said. "I did not presume to hope—now it is too late! Listen! I will tell you what I have told no living soul, though thereafter you may think me mad. Weak and humble as I am, I believe myself to have received a Divine mission. I believe that I shall execute it, or bring about its execution, but at the ultimate cost of my own life. Still, in such a service two are better than one. If you—can care enough—if you—"

But the lady had already turned away, and was murmuring her farewell in accents that sounded like a sob. Love and faith after this sort were not given to her.

Of all Owen's trials this was the sharpest. Of all his sacrifices this was the most complete.

CHAPTER III

THE TEMPTATION

Two years have gone by all but a few months, and from the rectory in a quiet English village we pass to a scene in Central, or South Central, Africa.

On the brow of a grassy slope dotted over with mimosa thorns, and close to a gushing stream of water, stands a house, or rather a hut, built of green brick and thatched with grass. Behind this hut is a fence of thorns, rough but strong, designed to protect all within it from the attacks of lions and other beasts of prey. At present, save for a solitary mule eating its provender by the wheel of a tented ox-waggon, it is untenanted, for the cattle have not yet been kraaled for the night. Presently Thomas Owen enters this enclosure by the back door of the hut, and having attended to the mule, which whinnies at the sight of him, goes to the gate and watches there till he sees his native boys driving the cattle up the slope of the hill. At length they arrive, and when he has counted them to make sure that none are missing, and in a few kind words commended the herds for their watchfulness, he walks to the front of the house and, seating himself upon a wooden stool set under a mimosa tree that grows near the door, he looks earnestly towards the west.

The man has changed somewhat since last we saw him. To begin with, he has grown a beard, and although the hot African sun has bronzed it into an appearance of health, his face is even thinner than it was, and therein the great spiritual eyes shine still more strangely.

At the foot of the slope runs a wide river, just here broken into rapids where the waters make an angry music. Beyond this river stretches a vast plain bounded on the horizon by mountain ranges, each line of them rising higher than the other till their topmost and more distant peaks melt imperceptibly into the tender blue of the heavens. This is the land of the Sons of Fire, and yonder amid the slopes of the nearest hills is the great kraal of their king, Umsuka, whose name, being interpreted, means The Thunderbolt.

In the very midst of the foaming rapids, and about a thousand yards from the house lies a space of rippling shallow water, where, unless it chances to be in flood, the river can be forded. It is this ford that Owen watches so intently.

"John should have been back twelve hours ago," he mutters to himself. "I pray that no harm has befallen him at the Great Place yonder."

Just then a tiny speck appears far away on the plain. It is a man travelling towards the water at a swinging trot. Going into the hut, Owen returns with a pair of field-glasses, and through them scrutinises the figure of the man.

"Heaven be praised! It is John," he mutters, with a sigh of relief. "Now, I wonder what answer he brings?"

Half an hour later John stands before him, a stalwart native of the tribe of the Amasuka, the People of Fire, and with uplifted hand salutes him, giving him titles of honour.

"Praise me not, John," said Owen; "praise God only, as I have taught you to do. Tell me, have you seen the king, and what is his word?"

"Father," he answered, "I journeyed to the great town, as you bade me, and I was admitted before the majesty of the king; yes, he received me in the courtyard of the House of Women. With his guards, who stood at a distance out of hearing, there were present three only; but oh! those three were great, the greatest in all the land after the king. They were Hafela, the king that is to come, the prince Nodwengo, his brother, and Hokosa the terrible, the chief of the wizards; and I tell you, father, that my blood dried up and my heart shrivelled when they turned their eyes upon me, reading the thoughts of my heart."

"Have I not told you, John, to trust in God, and fear nothing at the hands of man?"

"You told me, father, but still I feared," answered the messenger humbly. "Yet, being bidden to it, I lifted my forehead from the dust and stood upon my feet before the king, and delivered to him the message which you set between my lips."

"Repeat the message, John."

"'O King,' I said, 'beneath those footfall the whole earth shakes, whose arms stretch round the world and whose breath is the storm, I, whose name is John, am sent by the white man whose name is Messenger'—for by that title you bade me make you known—'who for a year has dwelt in the land that your spears have wasted beyond the banks of the river. These are the words which he spoke to me, O King, that I pass on to you with my tongue: "To the King Umsuka, lord of the Amasuka, the Sons of Fire, I, Messenger, who am the servant and the ambassador of the King of Heaven, give greeting. A year ago, King, I sent to you saying that the message which was brought by that white man whom you drove from your land had reached the ears of Him whom I serve, the High and Holy One, and that, speaking in my heart, He had commanded me to take up the challenge of your message. Here am I, therefore, ready to abide by the law which you have laid down; for if guile or lies be found in me, then let me travel from your land across the bridge of spears. Still, I would dwell a little while here where I am before I pass into the shadow of your rule and speak in the ears of your people as I have been bidden. Know, King, that first I would learn your tongue, and therefore I demand that one of your people may be sent to dwell with me and to teach me that tongue. King, you heard my words and you sent me a man to dwell with me, and that man has taught me your tongue, and I also have taught him, converting him to my faith and giving him a new name, the name of John. King, now I seek your leave to visit you, and to deliver into your ears the words with which I, Messenger, am charged. I have spoken."'

"Thus I, John, addressed the great ones, my father, and they listened in silence. When I had done they spoke together, a word here and a word there. Then Hokosa, the king's mouth, answered me, telling the thought of the king: 'You are a bold man, you whose name is John, but who once had another name—you, my servant, who dare to appear before me, and to make it known to me that you have been turned to a new faith and serve another king than I. Yet because you are bold, I forgive you. Go back now to that white man who is named Messenger and who comes upon an embassy to me from the Lord of Heaven, and bid him come in peace. Yet warn him once again that here also we know something of the Powers that are not seen, here also we have our wizards who draw wisdom from the air, who tame the thunderbolt and compel the rain, and that he must show himself greater than all of these if he would not pass hence by the bridge of spears. Let him, therefore, take counsel with his heart and with Him he serves, if such a One there is, and let him come or let him stay away as it shall please him.'"

"So be it," said Owen; "the words of the king are good, and to-morrow we will start for the Great Place."

John heard and assented, but without eagerness.

"My father," he said, in a doubtful and tentative voice, "would it not perhaps be better to bide here awhile first?"

"Why?" asked Owen. "We have sown, and now is the hour to reap."

"It is so, my father, but as I ran hither, full of the king's words, it came into my mind that now is not the time to convert the Sons of Fire. There is trouble brewing at the Great Palace, father. Listen, and I will tell you; as I have heard, so I will tell you. You know well that our King Umsuka has two sons, Hafela and Nodwengo; and of these Hafela is the heir-apparent, the fruit of the chief wife of the king, and Nodwengo is sprung from another wife. Now Hafela is proud and cruel, a warrior of warriors, a terrible man, and Nodwengo is gentle and mild, like to his mother whom the king loves. Of late it has been discovered that Hafela, weary of waiting for power, has made a plot to depose his father and to kill Nodwengo, his brother, so that the land and those who dwell in it may become his without question. This plot the king knows—I had it from one of his women, who is my sister—and he is very wroth, yet he dare do little, for he grows old and timid, and seeks rest, not war. Yet he is minded, if he can find the heart, to go back upon the law and to name Nodwengo as his heir before all the army at the feast of the first-fruits, which shall be held on the third day from to-night. This Hafela knows, and Nodwengo knows it also, and each of them has summoned his following, numbering thousands and tens of thousands of spears, to attend this feast of the first-fruits. That feast may well be a feast of vultures, my father, and when the brothers and their regiments rush together fighting for the throne, what will chance to the white man who comes at such a moment to preach a faith of peace, and to his servant, one John, who led him there?"

"I do not know," answered Owen, "and it troubles me not at all. I go to carry out my mission, and in this way or in that it will be carried out. John, if you are fearful or unbelieving leave me to go alone."

"Nay, father, I am not fearful; yet, father, I would have you understand. Yonder there are men who can work wizardry. Wow! I know, for I have seen it, and they will demand from you magic greater than their magic."

"What of it, John?"

"Only this, my father, that if they ask and you fail to give, they will kill you. You teach beautiful things, but say, are you a wizard? When the child of a woman yonder lay dead, you could not raise it as did the

Christ; when the oxen were sick with the pest, you could not cure them; or at least, my father, you did not, although you wept for the child and were sorry at the loss of the oxen. Now, my father, if perchance they ask you to do such things as these yonder, or die, say what will happen?"

"One of two things, John: either I shall die or I shall do the things."

"But"—hesitated John—"surely you do not believe that—" and he broke off.

Owen turned round and looked at his disciple with kindling eyes. "I do believe, O you of little faith!" he said. "I do believe that yonder I have a mission, and that He Whom I serve will give me power to carry out that mission. You are right, I can work no miracles; but He can work miracles Whom everything in heaven and earth obeys, and if there is need He will work them through me, His instrument. Or perhaps He will not work them, and I shall die, because thus His ends will best be forwarded. At the least I go in faith, fearing nothing, for what has he to fear who knows the will of God and does it? But to you who doubt, I say—leave me!"

The man spread out his hands in deprecation; his thick lips trembled a little, and something like a tear appeared at the corners of his eyes.

"Father," he said, "am I a coward that you should talk to me thus? I, who for twenty years have been a soldier of my king and for ten a captain in my regiment? These scars show whether or no I am a coward," and he pointed to his breast, "but of them I will not speak. I am no coward, else I had not gone upon that errand of yours. Why, then, should you reproach me because my ears are not so open as yours, as my heart has not understanding? I worship that God of Whom you have taught me, but He never speaks to me as He does to you. I never meet Him as I walk at night; He leaves me quite alone. Therefore it is that I fear that when the hour of trial comes He may desert you; and unless He covers you with His shield, of this I am sure, that the spear is forged which shall blush red in your heart, my father. It is for you that I fear, who are so gentle and tender; not for myself, who am well accustomed to look in the eyes of Death, and who expect no more than death."

"Forgive me," said Owen hastily, for he was moved; "and be sure that the shield will be over us till the time comes for us to pass whither we shall need none."

That night Owen rose from the task at which he was labouring slowly and painfully—a translation of passages from the Gospel of St. John into the language of the Amasuka—and going to the open window-place of the hut, he rested his elbows upon it and thought, staring with empty eyes into the blackness of the night. Now it was as he sat thus that a great agony of doubt took possession of his soul. The strength which hitherto had supported him seemed to be withdrawn, and he was left, as John had said, "quite alone." Strange voices seemed to whisper in his ears, reproaching and reviling him; temptations long ago trampled under foot rose again in might, alluring him.

"Fool," said the voices, "get you hence before it is too late. You have been mad; you who dreamed that for your sake, to satisfy your pride, the Almighty will break His silence and strain His law. Are you then better, or greater, or purer than millions who have gone before you, that for you and you alone this thing should be done? Why, were it not that you are mad, you would be among the chief of sinners; you who dare to ask that the Powers of Heaven should be set within your feeble hand, that the Angels of Heaven should wait upon your mortal breath. Worm that you are, has God need of such as you? If it is

His will to turn the heart of yonder people He will do it, but not by means of you. You and the servant whom you are deluding to his death will perish miserably, and this alone shall be the fruit of your presumptuous sin. Get you back out of this wilderness before the madness takes you afresh. You are still young, you have wealth; look where She stands yonder whom you desire. Get you back, and forget your folly in her arms."

These thoughts, and many others of like nature, tore Owen's soul in that hour of strange and terrible temptation. He seemed to see himself standing before the thousands of the savage nation he went to save, and to hear the mocking voices of their witch-finders commanding him, if he were a true man and the servant of that God of Whom he prated, to give them a sign, only a little sign; perhaps to move a stone without touching it with his hand, or to cause a dead bough to blossom.

Then he would beseech Heaven with frantic prayers, and in vain, till at length, amidst a roar of laughter, he, the false prophet and the liar, was led out to his doom. He saw the piteous wondering look of the believer whom he had betrayed to death; he saw the fierce faces and the spears on high. Seeing all this his spirit broke, and, just as the little clock in the room behind him struck the first stroke of midnight, with a great and bitter cry to God to give him back the faith and strength that he had lost, Owen's head fell forward and he sank into a swoon there upon the window-place.

CHAPTER IV

THE VISION

Was it swoon or sleep?

At least it seemed to Owen that presently once again he was gazing into the dense intolerable blackness of the night. Then a marvel came to pass, for the blackness opened, or rather on it, framed and surrounded by it, there appeared a vision. It was the vision of a native town, having a great bare space in the centre of it encircled by hundreds or thousands of huts. But there was no one stirring about the huts, for it was night—not this his night of trial indeed, since now the sky was strewn with innumerable stars. Everything was silent about that town, save that now and again a dog barked or a fretful child wailed within a hut, or the sentries as they passed saluted each other in the name of the king.

Among all those hundreds of huts, to Owen it seemed that his attention was directed to one which stood apart surrounded with a fence. Now the interior of the hut opened itself to him. It was not lighted, yet with his spirit sense he could see its every detail: the polished floor, the skin rugs, the beer gourds, the shields and spears, the roof-tree of red wood, and the dried lizard hanging from the thatch, a charm to ward off evil. In this hut, seated face to face halfway between the centre-post and the door-hole, were two men. The darkness was deep about them, and they whispered to each other through it; but in his dream this was no bar to Owen's sight. He could discern their faces clearly.

One of them was that of a man of about thirty-five years of age. In stature he was almost a giant. He wore a kaross of leopard skins, and on his wrists and ankles were rings of ivory, the royal ornaments. His face was fierce and powerful; his eyes, which were set far apart, rolled so much that at times they seemed all white; and his fingers played nervously with the handle of a spear that he carried in his right hand. His companion was of a different stamp; a person of more than fifty years, he was tall and spare in figure, with delicately shaped hands and feet. His hair and little beard were tinged with grey, his face was strikingly handsome, nervous and expressive, and his forehead both broad and high. But more remarkable still were his eyes, which shone with a piercing brightness, almost grey in colour, steady as the flame of a well-trimmed lamp, and so cold that they might have been precious stones set in the head of a statue.

"Must I then put your thoughts in words?" said this man in a clear quick whisper. "Well, so be it; for I weary of sitting here in the dark waiting for water that will not flow. Listen, Prince; you come to talk to me of the death of a king—is it not so? Nay do not start. Why are you affrighted when you hear upon the lips of another the plot that these many months has been familiar to your breast?"

"Truly, Hokosa, you are the best of wizards, or the worst," answered the great man huskily. "Yet this once you are mistaken," he added with a change of voice. "I came but to ask you for a charm to turn my father's heart—"

"To dust? Prince, if I am mistaken, why am I the best of wizards, or the worst, and why did your jaw drop and your face change at my words, and why do you even now touch your dry lips with your tongue? Yes, I know that it is dark here, yet some can see in it, and I am one of them. Ay, Prince, and I can see your mind also. You would be rid of your father: he has lived too long. Moreover his love turns to Nodwengo, the good and gentle; and perhaps—who can say?—it is even in his thought, when all his regiments are about him two days hence, to declare that you, Prince, are deposed, and that your brother, Nodwengo, shall be king in your stead. Now, Nodwengo you cannot kill; he is too well loved and too well guarded. If he died suddenly, his dead lips would call out 'Murder!' in the ears of all men; and, Prince, all eyes would turn to you, who alone could profit by his end. But if the king should chance to die—why he is old, is he not? and such things happen to the old. Also he grows feeble, and will not suffer the regiments to be doctored for war, although day by day they clamour to be led to battle; for he seeks to end his years in peace."

"I say that you speak folly," answered the prince with vehemence.

"Then, Son of the Great One, why should you waste time in listening to me? Farewell, Hafela the Prince, first-born of the king, who in a day to come shall carry the shield of Nodwengo; for he is good and gentle, and will spare your life—if I beg it of him."

Hafela stretched out his hand through the darkness, and caught Hokosa by the wrist.

"Stay," he whispered, "it is true. The king must die; for if he does not die within three days, I shall cease to be his heir. I know it through my spies. He is angry with me; he hates me, and he loves Nodwengo and the mother of Nodwengo. But if he dies before the last day of the festival, then that decree will never pass his lips, and the regiments will never roar out the name of Nodwengo as the name of the king to come. He must die, I tell you, Hokosa, and—by your hand."

"By my hand, Prince! Nay; what have you to offer me in return for such a deed as this? Have I not grown up in Umsuka's shadow, and shall I cut down the tree that shades me?"

"What have I to offer you? This: that next to myself you shall be the greatest in the land, Hokosa."

"That I am already, and whoever rules it, that I must always be. I, who am the chief of wizards; I, the reader of men's hearts; I, the hearer of men's thoughts! I, the lord of the air and the lightning; I, the invulnerable. If you would murder, Prince, then do the deed; do it knowing that I have your secret, and that henceforth you who rule shall be my servant. Nay, you forget that I can see in the dark; lay down that assegai, or, by my spirit, prince as you are, I will blast you with a spell, and your body shall be thrown to the kites, as that of one who would murder his king and father!"

The prince heard and shook, his cheeks sank in, the muscles of his great form seemed to collapse, and he grovelled on the floor of the hut.

"I know your magic," he groaned; "use it for me, not against me! What is there that I can offer you, who have everything except the throne, whereon you cannot sit, seeing that you are not of the blood-royal?"

"Think," said Hokosa.

For a while the prince thought, till presently his form straightened itself, and with a quick movement he lifted up his head.

"Is it, perchance, my affianced wife?" he whispered; "the lady Noma, whom I love, and who, according to our custom, I shall wed as the queen to be after the feast of first-fruits? Oh! say it not, Hokosa."

"I say it," answered the wizard. "Listen, Prince. The lady Noma is the only child of my blood-brother, my friend, with whom I was brought up, he who was slain at my side in the great war with the tribes of the north. She was my ward: she was more; for through her—ah! you know not how—I held my converse with the things of earth and air, the very spirits that watch us now in this darkness, Hafela. Thus it happened, that before ever she was a woman, her mind grew greater than the mind of any other woman, and her thought became my thought, and my thought became her thought, for I and no other am her master. Still I waited to wed her till she was fully grown; and while I waited I went upon an embassy to the northern tribes. Then it was that you saw the maid in visiting at my kraal, and her beauty and her wit took hold of you; and in the council of the king, as you have a right to do, you named her as your head wife, the queen to be.

"The king heard and bowed his head; he sent and took her, and placed her in the House of the Royal Women, there to abide till this feast of the first-fruits, when she shall be given to you in marriage. Yes, he sent her to that guarded house wherein not even I may set my foot. Although I was afar, her spirit warned me, and I returned, but too late; for she was sealed to you of the blood-royal, and that is a law which may not be broken.

"Hafela, I prayed you to return her to me, and you mocked me. I would have brought you to your death, but it could not have availed me: for then, by that same law, which may not be broken, she who was sealed to you must die with you; and though thereafter her spirit would sit with me till I died also, it was not enough, since I who have conquered all, yet cannot conquer the fire that wastes my heart, nor cease to long by night and day for a woman who is lost to me. Then it was, Hafela, that I plotted vengeance against you. I threw my spell over the mind of the king, till he learnt to hate you and your evil deeds; and I, even I, have brought it about that your brother should be preferred before you, and that you shall be the servant in his house. This is the price that you must pay for her of whom you have robbed me; and by my spirit and her spirit you shall pay! Yet listen. Hand back the girl, as you may do—for she is not yet your wife—and choose another for your queen, and I will undo all that I have done, and I will find you a means, Hafela, to carry out your will. Ay, before six suns have set, the regiments rushing past you shall hail you King of the Nation of the Amasuka, Lord of the ancient House of Fire!"

"I cannot," groaned the prince; "death were better than this!"

"Ay, death were better; but you shall not die, you shall live a servant, and your name shall become a mockery, a name for women to make rhymes on."

Now the prince sprang up.

"Take her!" he hissed; "take her! you, who are an evil ghost; you, beneath whose eyes children wail, and at whose passing the hairs on the backs of hounds stand up! Take her, priest of death and ill; but take my curse with her! Ah! I also can prophecy; and I tell you that this woman whom you have taught, this witch of many spells, whose glance can shrivel the hearts of men, shall give you to drink of your own medicine; ay, she shall dog you to the death, and mock you while you perish by an end of shame!"

"What," laughed the wizard, "have I a rival in my own arts? Nay, Hafela, if you would learn the trade, pay me well and I will give you lessons. Yet I counsel you not; for you are flesh, nothing but flesh, and he who would rule the air must cultivate the spirit. Why, I tell you, Prince, that even the love for her who is my heart, the lady whom we both would wed, partaking of the flesh as, alas! it does, has cost me half my powers. Now let us cease from empty scoldings, and strike our bargain.

"Listen. On the last day of the feast, when all the regiments are gathered to salute the king there in his Great Place according to custom, you shall stand forth before the king and renounce Noma, and she shall pass back to the care of my household. You yourself shall bring her to where I stand, and as I take her from you I will put into your hand a certain powder. Then you shall return to the side of the king, and after our fashion shall give him to drink the bowl of the first-fruits; but as you stir the beer, you will let fall into it that powder which I have given you. The king will drink, and what he leaves undrunk you will throw out upon the dust.

"Now he will rise to give out to the people his royal decree, whereby, Prince, you are to be deposed from your place as heir, and your brother, Nodwengo, is to be set in your seat. But of that decree never a word shall pass his lips; if it does, recall your saying and take back the lady Noma from where she stands beside me. I tell you that never a word will pass his lips; for even as he rises a stroke shall take him, such a stroke as often falls upon the fat and aged, and he will sink to the ground snoring through his nostrils. For a while thereafter—it may be six hours, it may be twelve—he shall lie insensible, and then a cry will arise that the king is dead!"

"Ay," said Hafela, "and that I have poisoned him!"

"Why, Prince? Few know what is in your father's mind, and with those, being king, you will be able to deal. Also this is the virtue of the poison which I choose, that it is swift, yet the symptoms of it are the symptoms of a natural sickness. But that your safety and mine may be assured, I have made yet another plan, though of this there will be little need. You were present two days since when a runner came from the white man who sojourns beyond our border, he who seeks to teach us, the Children of Fire, a new faith, and gives out that he is the messenger of the King of heaven. This runner asked leave for the white man to visit the Great Place, and, speaking in the king's name, I gave him leave. But I warned his servant that if his master came, a sign should be required of him to show that he was a true man, and had of the wisdom of the King of Heaven; and that if he failed therein, then that he should die as that white liar died who visited us in bygone years.

"Now I have so ordered that this white man, passing through the Valley of Death yonder, shall reach the Great Place not long before the king drinks of the cup of the first-fruits. Then if any think that something out of nature has happened to the king, they will surely think also that this strange prayer-doctor has wrought the evil. Then also I will call for a sign from the white man, praying of him to recover the king of his sickness; and when he fails, he shall be slain as a worker of spells and the false prophet of a false god, and so we shall be rid of him and his new faith, and you shall be cleared of doubt. Is not the plan good, Prince?"

"It is very good, Hokosa—save for one thing only."

"For what thing?"

"This: the white man who is named Messenger might chance to be a true prophet of a true God, and to recover the king."

"Oho, let him do it, if he can; but to do it, first he must know the poison and its antidote. There is but one, and it is known to me only of all men in this land. When he has done that, then I, yes, even I, Hokosa, will begin to inquire concerning this God of his, who shows Himself so mighty in person of His messenger." And he laughed low and scornfully.

"Prince, farewell! I go forth alone, whither you dare not follow at this hour, to seek that which we shall need. One word—think not to play me false, or to cheat me of my price; for whate'er betides, be sure of this, that hour shall be the hour of your dooming. Hail to you, Son of the King! Hail! and farewell." Then, removing the door-board, the wizard passed from the hut and was gone.

The vision changed. Now there appeared a valley walled in on either side with sloping cliffs of granite; a desolate place, sandy and, save for a single spring, without water, strewn with boulders of rock, some of them piled fantastically one upon the other. At a certain spot this valley widened out, and in the mouth of the space thus formed, midway between the curved lines of the receding cliffs, stood a little hill or koppie, also built up of boulders. It was a place of death; for all around the hill, and piled in hundreds between the crevices of its stones, lay the white bones of men.

Nor was this all. Its summit was flat, and in the midst of it stood a huge tree. Even had it not been for the fruit which hung from its branches, the aspect of that tree must have struck the beholder as uncanny, even as horrible. The bark on its great bole was leprous white; and from its gaunt and spreading rungs rose branches that subdivided themselves again and again, till at last they terminated in round green fingers, springing from grey, flat slabs of bark, in shape not unlike that of a human palm. Indeed, from a little distance this tree, especially if viewed by moonlight, had the appearance of bearing on it hundreds or thousands of the arms and hands of men, all of them stretched imploringly to Heaven.

Well might they seem to do so, seeing that to its naked limbs hung the bodies of at least twenty human beings who had suffered death by order of the king or his captains, or by the decree of the company of wizards, whereof Hokosa was the chief. There on the Hill of Death stood the Tree of Death; and that in its dank shade, or piled upon the ground beneath it, hung and lay the pitiful remnants of the multitudes who for generations had been led thither to their doom.

Now, in Owen's vision a man was seen approaching by the little pathway that ran up the side of the mount—the Road of Lost Footsteps it was called. It was Hokosa the wizard. Outside the circle of the tree he halted, and drawing a tanned skin from a bundle of medicines which he carried, he tied it about his mouth; for the very smell of that tree is poisonous and must not be suffered to reach the lungs.

Presently he was under the branches, where once again he halted; this time it was to gaze at the body of an old man which swung to and fro in the night breeze.

"Ah! friend," he muttered, "we strove for many years, but it seems that I have conquered at the last. Well, it is just; for if you could have had your way, your end would have been my end."

Then very leisurely, as one who is sure that he will not be interrupted, Hokosa began to climb the tree, till at length some of the green fingers were within his reach. Resting his back against a bough, one by one he broke off several of them, and averting his face so that the fumes of it might not reach him, he caused the thick milk-white juice that they contained to trickle into the mouth of a little gourd which was hung about his neck by a string. When he had collected enough of the poison and carefully corked the gourd with a plug of wood, he descended the tree again. At the great fork where the main branches sprang from the trunk, he stood a while contemplating a creeping plant which ran up them. It was a plant of naked stem, like the tree it grew upon; and, also like the tree, its leaves consisted of bunches of green spikes having a milky juice.

"Strange," he said aloud, "that Nature should set the bane and the antidote side by side, the one twined about the other. Well, so it is in everything; yes, even in the heart of man. Shall I gather some of this juice also? No; for then I might repent and save him, remembering that he has loved me, and thus lose her I seek, her whom I must win back or be withered. Let the messenger of the King of Heaven save him, if he can. This tree lies on his path; perchance he may prevail upon its dead to tell him of the bane and of the antidote." And once more the wizard laughed mockingly.

The vision passed. At this moment Thomas Owen, recovering from his swoon, lifted his head from the window-place. The night before him was as black as it had been, and behind him the little American clock was still striking the hour of midnight. Therefore he could not have remained insensible for longer than a few seconds.

A few seconds, yet how much he had seen in them. Truly his want of faith had been reproved—truly he also had been "warned of God in a dream,"—truly "his ears had been opened and his instruction sealed." His soul had been "kept back from the pit," and his life from "perishing by the sword;" and the way of the wicked had been made clear to him "in a dream, in a vision of the night when deep sleep falleth upon men."

Not for nothing had he endured that agony, and not for nothing had he struggled in the grip of doubt.

CHAPTER V

THE FEAST OF THE FIRST-FRUITS

On the third morning from this night whereof the strange events have been described, an ox-waggon might have been seen outspanned on the hither side of those ranges of hills that were visible from the river. These mountains, which although not high are very steep, form the outer barrier and defence of the kingdom of the Amasuka. Within five hundred yards of where the waggon stood, however, a sheer cliffed gorge, fire-riven and water-hewn, pierced the range, and looking on it, Owen knew it for the gorge of his dream. Night and day the mouth of it was guarded by a company of armed soldiers, whose huts were built high on outlook places in the mountains, whence their keen eyes could scan the vast expanses of plain. A full day before it reached them, they had seen the white-capped waggon crawling across the veldt, and swift runners had reported its advent to the king at his Great Place.

Back came the word of the king that the white man, with the waggon and his servant, were to be led on towards the Great Place at such speed as would bring him there in time for him to behold the last ceremony of the feast of first-fruits; but, for the present, that the waggon itself and the oxen were to be left at the mouth of the gorge, in charge of a guard, who would be answerable for them.

Now, on this morning the captain of the guard and his orderlies advanced to the waggon and stood in front of it. They were splendid men, armed with great spears and shields, and adorned with feather head-dresses and all the wild finery of their regiment. Owen descended from the waggon and came to meet them, and so for a few moments they remained, face to face, in silence. A strange contrast they presented as they stood there; the bare-headed white man frail, delicate, spiritual of countenance, and the warriors great, grave, powerful, a very embodiment of the essence of untamed humanity, an incarnate presentation of the spirit of savage warfare.

"How are you named, White Man?" asked the captain.

"Chief, I am named Messenger."

"The peace of the king be with you, Messenger," said the captain, lifting his spear.

"The peace of God be with you, Chief," answered Owen, holding up his hands in blessing.

"Who is God?" asked the captain.

"Chief, He is the King I serve, and His word is between my lips."

"Then pass on, Messenger of God, and deliver the word of God your King into the ears of my king, at his Great Place yonder. Pass on riding the beast you have brought with you, for the way is rough; but your waggon, your oxen, and your servants, save this man only who is of the Children of Fire, must stay here in my keeping. Fear not, Messenger, I will hold them safe."

"I do not fear, Chief, there is honour in your eyes."

Some hours later, Owen, mounted on his mule, was riding through the gorge, a guard in front of and behind him, and with them carriers who had been sent to bear his baggage. At his side walked his disciple John, and his face was sad.

"Why are you still afraid?" asked Owen.

"Ah! father, because this is a place of fear. Here in this valley men are led to die; presently you will see."

"I have seen," answered Owen. "Yonder where we shall halt is a mount, and on that mount stands a tree; it is called the Tree of Death, and it stretches a thousand hands to Heaven, praying for mercy that does not come, and from its boughs there hangs fruit, a fruit of dead men—yes, twenty of them hang there this day."

"How know you these things, my father," asked the man amazed, "seeing that I have never spoken to you of them?"

"Nay," he answered, "God has spoken to me. My God and your God."

Another hour passed, and they were resting by the spring of water, near to the shadow of the dreadful tree, for in that gorge the sun burned fiercely. John counted the bodies that swung upon it, and again looked fearfully at Owen, for there were twenty of them.

"I desire to go up to that tree," Owen said to the guard.

"As you will, Messenger," answered their leader; "I have no orders to prevent you from so doing. Still," he added with a solemn smile, "it is a place that few seek of their own will, and, because I like you well, Messenger, I pray it may never be my duty to lead you there of the king's will."

Then Owen went up to the tree and John with him, only John would not pass beneath the shadow of its branches; but stood by wondering, while his master bound a handkerchief about his mouth.

"How did he know that the breath of the tree is poisonous?" John wondered.

Owen walked to the bole of the tree, and breaking off some of the finger-like leaves of the creeper that twined about it, he pressed their milky juice into a little bottle that he had made ready. Then he returned quickly, for the sights and odours of the place were not to be borne.

Outside the circle of the branches he halted, and removed the handkerchief from his mouth.

"Be of good cheer," he said to John, "and if it should chance that I am called away before my words come true, yet remember my words. I tell you that this Tree of Death shall become the Tree of Life for all the children of your people. Look! there above you is its sign and promise."

John lifted his eyes, following the line of Owen's outstretched hand, and saw this. High up upon the tree, and standing clear of all the other branches, was one straight, dead limb, and from this dead limb two arms projected at right angles, also dead and snapped off short. Had a carpenter fashioned a cross of wood and set it there, its proportions could not have been more proper and exact. It was very strange to find this symbol of the Christian hope towering above that place of human terror, and stranger still was the purpose which it must serve in a day to come.

Owen and John returned to the guard in silence, and presently they set forward on their journey. At length, passing beneath a natural arch of rock, they were out of the Valley of Death, and before them, not five hundred paces away, appeared the fence of the Great Place.

This Great Place stood upon a high plateau, in the lap of the surrounding hills, all of which were strongly fortified with schanses, pitfalls, and rough walls of stone. That plateau may have measured fifteen miles in circumference, and the fence of the town itself was about four miles in circumference. Within the fence and following its curve, for it was round, stood thousands of dome-shaped huts carefully set out in streets. Within these again was a stout stockade of timber, enclosing a vast arena of trodden earth, large enough to contain all the cattle of the People of Fire in times of danger, and to serve as a review ground for their impis in times of peace or festival.

At the outer gate of the kraal there was a halt, while the keepers of the gate despatched a messenger to their king to announce the advent of the white man. Of this pause Owen took advantage to array himself in the surplice and hood which he had brought with him in readiness for that hour. Then he gave the mule to John to lead behind him.

"What do you, Messenger?" asked the leader of the guard, astonished.

"I clothe myself in my war-dress," he answered.

"Where then is your spear, Messenger?"

"Here," said Owen, presenting to his eyes a crucifix of ivory, most beautifully carved.

"I perceive that you are of the family of wizards," said the man, and fell back.

Now they entered the kraal and passed for three hundred yards or more through rows of huts, till they reached the gate of the stockade, which was opened to them. Once within it, Owen saw a wonderful sight, such a sight as few white men have seen. The ground of the enormous oval before him was not flat. Either from natural accident or by design it sloped gently upwards, so that the spectator, standing by the gate or at the head of it before the house of the king, could take in its whole expanse, and, if his sight were keen enough, could see every individual gathered there.

On the particular day of Owen's arrival it was crowded with regiments, twelve of them, all dressed in their different uniforms and bearing shields to match, not one of which was less than 2500 strong. At this moment the regiments were massed in deep lines, each battalion by itself, on either side of the broad roadway that ran straight up the kraal to where the king, his sons, his advisers and guards, together with the company of wizards, were placed in front of the royal house.

There they stood in absolute silence, like tens of thousands of bronze statues, and Owen perceived that either they were resting or that they were gathered thus to receive him. That the latter was the case soon became evident, for as he appeared, a white spot at the foot of the slope, countless heads turned and myriads of eyes fastened themselves upon him. For an instant he was dismayed; there was something terrifying in this numberless multitude of warriors, and the thought of the task that he had undertaken crushed his spirit. Then he remembered, and shaking off his fear and doubt, alone, save for his disciple John, holding the crucifix aloft, he walked slowly up the wide road towards the place where he guessed that the king must be. His arm was weary ere ever he reached it, but at length he found himself standing before a thickset old man, who was clad in leopard skins and seated upon a stool of polished wood.

"It is the king," whispered John behind him.

"Peace be to you," said Owen, breaking the silence.

"The wish is good, may it be fulfilled," answered the king in a deep voice, sighing as he said the words. "Yet yours is a strange greeting," he added. "Whence came you, White Man, how are you named, and what is your mission to me and to my people?"

"King, I come from beyond the sea; I am named Messenger, and my mission is to deliver to you the saying of God, my King and—yours."

At these words a gasp of astonishment went up from those who stood within hearing, expecting as they did to see them rewarded by instant death. But Umsuka only said:—

"'My King and yours'? Bold words, Messenger. Where then is this King to whom I, Umsuka, should bow the knee?"

"He is everywhere—in the heavens, on the earth, and below the earth."

"If He is everywhere, then He is here. Show me the likeness of this King, Messenger."

"Behold it," Owen answered, thrusting forward the crucifix.

Now all the great ones about the king stared at this figure of a dying man crowned with thorns and hanging on a cross, and then drew up their lips to laugh. But that laugh never left them; a sudden impulse, a mysterious wave of feeling choked it in their throats. A sense of the strangeness of the contrast between themselves in their armed multitudes and this one white-robed man in his loneliness took hold of them, and with it another sense of something not far removed from fear.

"A wizard indeed," they thought in their hearts, and what they thought the king uttered.

"I perceive," he said, "that you are either mad, White Man, or you are a prince of wizards. Mad you do not seem to be, for your eyes are calm, therefore a wizard you must be. Well, stand behind me: by-and-by I will hear your message and ask of you to show me your powers; but before then there are things which I must do. Are the lads ready? Ho, you, loose the bull!"

At the command a line of soldiers moved from the right, forming itself up in front of the king and his attendants, revealing a number of youths, of from sixteen to seventeen years of age, armed with sticks only, who stood in companies outside a massive gate. Presently this gate was opened, and through it, with a mad bellow, rushed a wild buffalo bull. On seeing them the brute halted, and for a few moments stood pawing the earth and tearing it with its great horns. Then it put down its head and charged. Instead of making way for it, uttering a shrill whistling sound, the youths rushed at the beast, striking with their sticks.

Another instant, and one of them appeared above the heads of his companions, thrown high into the air, to be followed by a second and a third. Now the animal was through the throng and carrying a poor boy on its horn, whence presently he fell dead; through and through the ranks of the regiments it charged furiously backward and forward.

Watching it fascinated, Owen noted that it was a point of honour for no man to stir before its rush; there they stood, and if the bull gored them, there they fell. At length, exhausted and terrified, the brute headed back straight up the lane where the main body of the youths were waiting for it. Now it was among them, and, reckless of wounds or death, they swarmed about it like bees, seizing it by legs, nose, horns and tail, till with desperate efforts they dragged it to the ground and beat the life out of it with their sticks. This done, they formed up before the king and saluted him.

"How many are killed?" he asked.

"Eight in all," was the answer, "and fifteen gored."

"A good bull," he said with a smile; "that of last year killed but five. Well, the lads fought him bravely. Let the dead be buried, the hurt tended, or, if their harms are hopeless, slain, and to the rest give a double ration of beer. Ho, now, fall back, men, and make a space for the Bees and the Wasps to fight in."

Some orders were given and a great ring was formed, leaving an arena clear that may have measured a hundred and fifty yards in diameter. Then suddenly, from opposite sides, the two regiments, known as the Bees and the Wasps respectively, rushed upon each other, uttering their war-cries.

"I put ten head of cattle on the Bees; who wagers on the Wasps?" cried the king.

"I, Lord," answered the Prince Hafela, stepping forward.

"You, Prince!" said the king with a quick frown. "Well, you are right to back them, they are your own regiment. Ah! they are at it."

By this time the scene was that of a hell broken loose upon the earth. The two regiments, numbering some 5000 men in all, had come together, and the roar of their meeting shields was like the roar of thunder. They were armed with kerries only, and not with spears, for the fight was supposed to be a mimic one; but these weapons they used with such effect that soon hundreds of them were down dead or with shattered skulls and bruised limbs. Fiercely they fought, while the whole army watched, for their rivalry was keen and for many months they had known that they were to be pitted one against the other on this day. Fiercely they fought, while the captains cried their orders, and the dust rose up in clouds as they swung to and fro, breast thrusting against breast. At length the end came; the Bees began to give, they fell back ever more quickly till their retreat was a rout, and, leaving many stretched upon the ground, amid the mocking cries of the army they were driven to the fence, by touching which they obtained peace at the hands of their victors.

The king saw, and his somewhat heavy, quiet face grew alive with rage.

"Search and see," he said, "if the captain of the Bees is alive and unhurt."

Messengers went to do his bidding, and presently they returned, bringing with them a man of magnificent appearance and middle age, whose left arm had been broken by a blow from a kerry. With his right hand he saluted first the king, then the Prince Nodwengo, a kindly-faced, mild-eyed man, in whose command he was.

"What have you to say?" asked the king, in a cold voice of anger. "Know you that you have cost me ten head of the royal white cattle?"

"King, I have nothing to say," answered the captain calmly, "except that my men are cowards."

"That is certainly so," said the king. "Let all the wounded among them be carried away; and for you, captain, who turn my soldiers into cowards, you shall die a dog's death, hanging to-morrow on the Tree of Doom. As for your regiment, I banish it to the fever country, there to hunt elephants for three years, since it is not fit to fight with men."

"It is well," replied the captain, "since death is better than shame. Only King, I have done you good service in the past; I ask that it may be presently and by the spear."

"So be it," said the king.

"I crave his life, father," said the Prince Nodwengo; "he is my friend."

"A prince should not choose cowards for his friends," replied the king; "let him be killed, I say."

Then Owen, who had been watching and listening, his heart sick with horror, stood forward and said:—

"King, in the name of Him I serve, I conjure you to spare this man and those others that are hurt, who have done no crime except to be driven back by soldiers stronger than themselves."

"Messenger," answered the king, "I bear with you because you are ignorant. Know that, according to our customs, this crime is the greatest of crimes, for here we show no mercy to the conquered."

"Yet you should do so," said Owen, "seeing that you also must ere long be conquered by death, and then how can you expect mercy who have shown none?"

"Let him be killed!" said the king.

"King!" cried Owen once more, "do this deed, and I tell you that before the sun is down great evil will overtake you."

"Do you threaten me, Messenger? Well, we will see. Let him be killed, I say."

Then the man was led away; but, before he went he found time to thank Owen and Nodwengo the prince, and to call down good fortune upon them.

CHAPTER VI

THE DRINKING OF THE CUP

Now the king's word was done, the anger went out of his eyes, and once more his countenance grew weary. A command was issued, and, with the most perfect order, moving like one man, the regiments changed their array, forming up battalion upon battalion in face of the king, that they might give him the royal salute so soon as he had drunk the cup of the first-fruits.

A herald stood forward and cried:—

"Hearken, you Sons of Fire! Hearken, you Children of Umsuka, Shaker of the Earth! Have any of you a boon to ask of the king?"

Men stood forward, and having saluted, one by one asked this thing or that. The king heard their requests, and as he nodded or turned his head away, so they were granted or refused.

When all had done, the Prince Hafela came forward, lifted his spear, and cried:—

"A boon, King!"

"What is it?" asked his father, eyeing him curiously.

"A small matter, King," he replied. "A while ago I named a certain woman, Noma, the ward of Hokosa the wizard, and she was sealed to me to fill the place of my first wife, the queen that is to be. She passed into the House of the Royal Women, and, by your command, King, it was fixed that I should marry her according to our customs to-morrow, after the feast of the first-fruits is ended. King, my heart is changed towards that woman; I no longer desire to take her to wife, and I pray that you will order that she shall now be handed back to Hokosa her guardian."

"You blow hot and cold with the same mouth, Hafela," said Umsuka, "and in love or war I do not like such men. What have you to say to this demand, Hokosa?"

Now Hokosa stepped forward from where he stood at the head of the company of wizards. His dress, like that of his companions, was simple, but in its way striking. On his shoulders he wore a cloak of shining snakeskin; about his loins was a short kilt of the same material; and round his forehead, arms and knees were fillets of snakeskin. At his side hung his pouch of medicines, and in his hand he held no spear, but a wand of ivory, whereof the top was roughly carved so as to resemble the head of a cobra reared up to strike.

"King," he said, "I have heard the words of the prince, and I do not think that this insult should have been put upon the Lady Noma, my ward, or upon me, her guardian. Still, let it be, for I would not that one should pass from under the shadow of my house whither she is not welcome. Without my leave the prince named this woman as his queen, as he had the right to do; and without my leave he unnames her, as he has the right to do. Were the prince a common man, according to custom he should pay a fine of cattle to be held by me in trust for her whom he discards; but this is a matter that I leave to you, King."

"You do well, Hokosa," answered Umsuka, "to leave this to me. Prince, you would not wish the fine that you should pay to be that of any common man. With the girl shall be handed over two hundred head of cattle. More, I will do justice: unless she herself consents, she shall not be put away. Let the Lady Noma be summoned."

Now the face of Hafela grew sullen, and watching, Owen saw a swift change pass over that of Hokosa. Evidently he was not certain of the woman. Presently there was a stir, and from the gates of the royal house the Lady Noma appeared, attended by women, and stood before the king. She was a tall and lovely girl, and the sunlight flashed upon her bronze-hued breast and her ornaments of ivory. Her black hair was fastened in a knot upon her neck, her features were fine and small, her gait was delicate and sure as that of an antelope, and her eyes were beautiful and full of pride. There she stood before the king, looking round her like a stag. Seeing her thus, Owen understood how it came about that she held two men so strangely different in the hollow of her hand, for her charm was of a nature to appeal to both of them—a charm of the spirit as well as of the flesh. And yet the face was haughty, a face that upon occasion might even become cruel.

"You sent for me and I am here, O King," she said, in a slow and quiet voice.

"Listen, girl," answered the king. "A while ago the Prince Hafela, my son, named you as her who should be his queen, whereon you were taken and placed in the House of the Royal Women, to abide the day of your marriage, which should be to-morrow."

"It is true that the prince has honoured me thus, and that you have been pleased to approve of his choice," she said, lifting her eyebrows. "What of it, O King?"

"This, girl: the prince who was pleased to honour you is now pleased to dishonour you. Here, in the presence of the council and army, he prays of me to annul his sealing to you, and to send you back to the house of your guardian, Hokosa the wizard."

Noma started, and her face grew hard.

"Is it so?" she said. "Then it would seem that I have lost favour in the eyes of my lord the prince, or that some fairer woman has found it."

"Of these matters I know nothing," replied the king; "but this I know, that if you seek justice you shall have it. Say but the word, and he to whom you were promised in marriage shall take you in marriage, whether he wills or wills it not."

At this speech, the face of Hafela was suddenly lit up as with the fire of hope, while over that of Hokosa there passed another subtle change. The girl glanced at them both and was silent for a while. Her breast heaved and her white teeth bit upon her lip. To Owen, who noted all, it was clear that rival passions were struggling in her heart: the passion of power and the passion of love, or of some emotion which he did not understand. Hokosa fixed his calm eyes upon her with a strange intensity of gaze, and while he gazed his form quivered with a suppressed excitement, much as a snake quivers that is about to strike its prey. To the careless eye there was nothing remarkable about his look and attitude; to the observer it was evident that both were full of extraordinary purpose. He was talking to the girl, not with words, but in some secret language that he and she understood alone. She started as one starts who catches the tone of a well-remembered voice in a crowd of strangers, and lifting her eyes from the ground, whither she had turned them in meditation, she looked up at Hokosa.

Instantly her face began to change. The haughtiness and anger went out of it, it grew troubled, the lips parted in a sigh. First she bent her head and body towards him, then without more ado she walked to where he stood and took him by the hand. Here, at some whispered word or sign, she seemed to recover herself, and again resuming the character of a proud offended beauty, she curtseyed to Umsuka, and spoke:—

"O King, as you see, I have made my choice. I will not force myself upon a man who scorns me, no, not even to share his place and power, though it is true that I love them both. Nay, I will return to Hokosa my guardian, and to his wife, Zinti, who has been as my mother, and with them be at peace."

"It is well," said the king, "and perhaps, girl, your choice is wise; perhaps your loss is not so great as you have thought. Hafela, take you the hand of Hokosa and release the girl back to him according to the law, promising in the ears of men before the first month of winter to pay him two hundred head of cattle as forfeit, to be held by him in trust for the girl."

In a sullen voice, his lips trembling with rage, Hafela did as the king commanded; and when the hands of the conspirators unclasped, Owen perceived that in that of the prince lay a tiny packet.

"Mix me the cup of the first-fruits, and swiftly," said the king again, "for the sun grows low in the heavens, and ere it sinks I have words to say."

Now a polished gourd filled with native beer was handed to Nodwengo, the second son of the king, and one by one the great councillors approached, and, with appropriate words, let fall into it offerings emblematic of fertility and increase. The first cast in a grain of corn; the second, a blade of grass; the third, a shaving from an ox's horn; the fourth, a drop of water; the fifth, a woman's hair; the sixth, a particle of earth; and so on, until every ingredient was added to it that was necessary to the magic brew.

Then Hokosa, as chief of the medicine men, blessed the cup according to the ancient forms, praying that he whose body was the heavens, whose eyes were lightning, and whose voice was thunder, the spirit whom they worshipped, might increase and multiply to them during the coming year all those fruits and elements that were present in the cup, and that every virtue which they contained might comfort the body of the king.

His prayer finished, it was the turn of Hafela to play his part as the eldest born of the king. Kneeling over the cup which stood upon the ground, a spear was handed to him that had been made red hot in the fire. Taking the spear, he stabbed with it towards the four quarters of the horizon; then, muttering some invocation, he plunged it into the bowl, stirring its contents till the iron grew black. Now he threw aside the spear, and lifting the bowl in both hands, he carried it to his father and offered it to him.

Although he had been unable to see him drop the poison into the cup, a glance at Hafela told Owen that it was there; for though he kept his face under control, he could not prevent his hands from twitching or the sweat from starting upon his brow and breast.

The king rose, and taking the bowl, held it on high, saying:—

"In this cup, which I drink on behalf of the nation, I pledge you, my people."

It was the signal for the royal salute, for which each regiment had been prepared. As the last word left the king's lips, every one of the thirty thousand men present in that great place began to rattle his kerry against the surface of his ox-hide shield. At first the sound produced resembled that of the murmur of the sea; but by slow and just degrees it grew louder and ever louder, till the roar of it was like the deepest voice of thunder, a sound awe-inspiring, terrible.

Suddenly, when its volume was most, four spears were thrown into the air, and at this signal every man ceased to beat upon his shield. In the place itself there was silence, but from the mountains around the echoes still crashed and volleyed. When the last of them had died away, the king brought the cup to the level of his lips. Owen saw, and knowing its contents, was almost moved to cry out in warning. Indeed, his arm was lifted and his mouth was open, when by chance he noted Hokosa watching him, and remembered. To act now would be madness, his time had not yet come.

The cup touched the king's lips, and at the sign from every throat in that countless multitude sprang the word "King!" and every foot stamped upon the ground, shaking the solid earth. Thrice the monarch drank, and thrice this tremendous salute, the salute of the whole nation to its ruler, was repeated, each time more loudly than the last. Then pouring the rest of the liquor on the ground, Umsuka set aside the cup, and in the midst of a silence that seemed deep after the crash of the great salute, he began to address the multitude:—

"Hearken, Councillors and Captains, and you, my people, hearken. As you know, I have two sons, calves of the Black Bull, princes of the land—my son Hafela, the eldest born, and my son Nodwengo, his half-brother—"

At this point the king began to grow confused. He hesitated, passing his hand over his eyes, then slowly and with difficulty repeated those words which he had already said.

"We hear you, Father," cried the councillors in encouragement, as for the second time he paused. While they still spoke, the veins in the king's neck were seen to swell suddenly, foam flecked with blood burst from his lips, and he fell headlong to the ground.

CHAPTER VII

THE RECOVERY OF THE KING

For a moment there was silence, then a great cry arose—a cry of "Our father is dead!" Presently with it were mingled other and angrier shouts of "The king is murdered!" and "He is bewitched, the white wizard has bewitched the king! He prophesied evil upon him, and now he has bewitched him!"

Meanwhile the captains and councillors formed a ring about Umsuka, and Hokosa bending over him examined him.

"Princes and Councillors," he said presently, "your father yet lives, but his life is like the life of a dying fire and soon he must be dead. This is sure, that one of two things has befallen him: either the heat has caused the blood to boil in his veins and he is smitten with a stroke from heaven, such as men who are fat and heavy sometimes die of; or he has been bewitched by a wicked wizard. Yonder stands one," and he pointed to Owen, "who not an hour ago prophesied that before the sun was down great evil should overtake the king. The sun is not yet down, and great evil has overtaken him. Perchance, Princes and Councillors, this white prophet can tell us of the matter."

"Perchance I can," answered Owen calmly.

"He admits it!" cried some. "Away with him!"

"Peace!" said Owen, holding the crucifix towards those whose spears threatened his life.

They shrank back, for this symbol of a dying man terrified them who could not guess its significance.

"Peace," went on Owen, "and listen. Be sure of this, Councillors, that if I die, your king will die; whereas if I live, your king may live. You ask me of this matter. Where shall I begin? Shall I begin with the tale of two men seated together some nights ago in a hut so dark that no eyes could see in it, save perchance the eyes of a wizard? What did they talk of in that hut, and who were those men? They talked, I think, of the death of a king and of the crowning of a king. They talked of a price to be paid for a certain medicine; and one of them had a royal air, and one—"

"Will ye hearken to this wild babbler while your king lies dying before your eyes?" broke in Hokosa, in a shrill, unnatural voice; for almost palsied with fear as he was at Owen's mysterious words, he still retained his presence of mind. "Listen now: what is he, and what did he say? He is one who comes hither to preach a new faith to us; he comes, he says, on an embassy from the King of Heaven, who has power over all things, and who, so these white men preach, can give power to His servants. Well, let this one cease prating and show us his strength, as he has been warned he would be called upon to do. Let him give us a sign. There before you lies your king, and he is past the help of man; even I cannot help him. Therefore, let this messenger cure him, or call upon his God to cure him; that seeing, we may know him to be a true messenger, and one sent by that King of whom he speaks. Let him do this now before our eyes, or let him perish as a wizard who has bewitched the king. Do you hear my words, Messenger, and can you draw this one back from between the Gates of Death?"

"I hear them," answered Owen quietly; "and I can—or if I cannot, then I am willing to pay the penalty with my life. You who are a doctor say that your king is as one who is already dead, so that whatever I may do I cannot hurt him further. Therefore I ask this of you, that you stand round and watch, but molest me neither by word nor deed while I attempt his cure. Do you consent?"

"It is just; we consent," said the councillors. "Let us see what the white man can do, and by the issue let him be judged." But Hokosa stared at Owen wondering, and made no answer.

"Bring some clean water to me in a gourd," said Owen.

It was brought and given to him. He looked round, searching the faces of those about him. Presently his eye fell upon the Prince Nodwengo, and he beckoned to him, saying:—

"Come hither, Prince, for you are honest, and I would have you to help me, and no other man."

The prince stepped forward and Owen gave him the gourd of water. Then he drew out the little bottle wherein he had stored the juice of the creeper, and uncorking it, he bade Nodwengo fill it up with water. This done, he clasped his hands, and lifting his eyes to heaven, he prayed aloud in the language of the Amasuka.

"O God," he prayed, "upon whose business I am here, grant, I beseech Thee, that by Thy Grace power may be given to me to work this miracle in the face of these people, to the end that I may win them to cease from their iniquities, to believe upon Thee, the only true God, and to save their souls alive. Amen."

Having finished his prayer, he took the bottle and shook it; then he commanded Nodwengo to sit upon the ground and hold his father's head upon his knee. Now, as all might see by many signs, the king was upon the verge of death, for his lips were purple, his breathing was rare and stertorous, and his heart stood well-nigh still.

"Open his mouth and hold down the tongue," said Owen.

The prince obeyed, pressing down the tongue with a snuff spoon. Then placing the neck of the bottle as far into the throat as it would reach, Owen poured the fluid it contained into the body of the king, who made a convulsive movement and instantly seemed to die.

"He is dead," said one; "away with the false prophet!"

"It may be so, or it may not be so," answered Owen. "Wait for the half of an hour; then, if he shows no sign of life, do what you will with me."

"It is well," they said; "so be it."

Slowly the minutes slipped by, while the king lay like a corpse before them, and outside of that silent ring the soldiers murmured as the wind. The sun was sinking fast, and Hokosa watched it, counting the seconds. At length he spoke:—

"The half of the hour that you demanded is dead, White Man, as dead as the king; and now the time has come for you to die also," and he stretched out his hand to take him.

Owen looked at his watch and replied:—

"There is still another minute; and you, Hokosa, who are skilled in medicines, may know that this antidote does not work so swiftly as the bane."

The shot was a random one, but it told, for Hokosa fell back and was silent.

The seconds passed on as the minute hand of the watch went round from ten to twenty, from twenty to thirty, from thirty to forty. A few more instants and the game was played. Had that dream of his been vain imagining, and was all his faith nothing but a dream wondered Owen? Well, if so, it would be best that he should die. But he did not believe that it was so; he believed that the Power above him would intervene to save—not him, indeed, but all this people.

"Let us make an end," said Hokosa, "the time is done."

"Yes," said Owen, "the time is done—and the king lives!"

Even as he spoke the pulses in the old man's forehead were seen to throb, and the veins in his neck to swell as they had swollen after he had swallowed the poison; then once more they shrank to their natural size. Umsuka stirred a hand, groaned, sat up, and spoke:—

"What has chanced to me?" he said. "I have descended into deep darkness, now once again I see light."

No one answered, for all were staring, terrified and amazed, at the Messenger—the white wizard to whom had been given power to bring men back from the gate of death. At length Owen said:—

"This has chanced to you, King: that evil which I prophesied to you if you refused to listen to the voice of mercy has fallen upon you. By now you would have been dead, had it not pleased Him Whom I serve, working through me, His messenger, to bring you back to look upon the sun. Thank Him, therefore, and worship Him, for He alone is Master of the Earth," and he held the crucifix before his eyes.

The humbled monarch lifted his hand—he who for many years had made obeisance to none—and saluted the symbol, saying:—

"Messenger, I thank Him and I worship Him, though I know Him not. Say now, how did His magic work upon me to make me sick to death and to recover me?"

"By the hand of man, King, and by the virtues that lie hid in Nature. Did you not drink of a cup, and were not many things mixed in the draught? Was it not but now in your mind to speak words that should bring down the head of pride and evil, and lift up the head of truth and goodness?"

"O White Man, how know you these things?" gasped the king.

"I know them, it is enough. Say, who was it that stirred the bowl, King, and who gave you to drink?"

Now Umsuka staggered to his feet, and cried aloud in a voice that was thick with rage:—

"By my head and the heads of my fathers I smell the plot! My son, the Prince Hafela, has learned my counsel, and would have slain me before I said words that should set him beneath the feet of Nodwengo. Seize him, captains, and let him be brought before me for judgment!"

Men looked this way and that to carry out the command of the king, but Hafela was gone. Already he was upon the hillside, running as a man has rarely run before—his face set towards that fastness in the mountains where he could find refuge among his mother's tribesmen and the regiments which he commanded. Of late they had been sent thither by the king that they might be far from the Great Place when their prince was disinherited.

"He is fled," said one; "I saw him go."

"Pursue him and bring him back, dead or alive!" thundered the king. "A hundred head of cattle to the man who lays hand upon him before he reaches the impi of the North, for they will fight for him!"

"Stay!" broke in Owen. "Once before this day I prayed of you, King, to show mercy, and you refused it. Will you refuse me a second time? Leave him his life who has lost all else."

"That he may rebel against me? Well, White Man, I owe you much, and for this time your wisdom shall be my guide, though my heart speaks against such gentleness. Hearken, councillors and people, this is my decree: that Hafela, my son, who would have murdered me, be deposed from his place as heir to my throne, and that Nodwengo, his brother, be set in that place, to rule the People of Fire after me when I die."

"It is good, it is just!" said the council. "Let the king's word be done."

"Hearken again," said Umsuka. "Let this white man, who is named Messenger, be placed in the House of Guests and treated with all honour; let oxen be given him from the royal herds and corn from the granaries, and girls of noble blood for wives if he wills them. Hokosa, into your hand I deliver him, and, great though you are, know this, that if but a hair of his head is harmed, with your goods and your life you shall answer for it, you and all your house."

"Let the king's word be done," said the councillors again.

"Heralds," went on Umsuka, "proclaim that the feast of the first-fruits is ended, and my command is that every regiment should seek its quarters, taking with it a double gift of cattle from the king, who has been saved alive by the magic of this white man. And now, Messenger, farewell, for my head grows weary. To-morrow I will speak with you."

Then the king was led away into the royal house, and save those who were quartered in it, the regiments passed one by one through the gates of the kraal, singing their war-songs as they went. Darkness fell upon the Great Place, and through it parties of men might be seen dragging thence the corpses of those who had fallen in the fight with sticks, or been put to death thereafter by order of the king.

"Messenger," said Hokosa, bowing before Owen, "be pleased to follow me." Then he led him to a little kraal numbering five or six large and beautifully made huts, which stood by itself, within its own fence, at the north end of the Great Place, not far from the house of the king. In front of the centre hut a fire was burning, and by its light women appeared cleaning out the huts and bringing food and water.

"Here you may rest in safety, Messenger," said Hokosa, "seeing that night and day a guard from the king's own regiment will stand before your doors."

"I do not need them," answered Owen, "for none can harm me till my hour comes. I am a stranger here and you are a great man; yet, Hokosa, which of us is the safest this night?"

"Your meaning?" said Hokosa sharply.

"O man!" answered Owen, "when in a certain hour you crept up the valley yonder, and climbing the Tree of Death gathered its poison, went I not with you? When, before that hour, you sat in yonder hut bargaining with the Prince Hafela—the death of a king for the price of a girl—was I not with you? Nay, threaten me not—in your own words I say it—'lay down that assegai, or by my spirit your body shall be thrown to the kites, as that of one who would murder the king'—and the king's guest!"

"White Man," whispered Hokosa throwing down the spear, "how can these things be? I was alone in the hut with the prince, I was alone beneath the Tree of Doom, and you, as I know well, were beyond the river. Your spies must be good, White Man."

"My spirit is my only spy, Hokosa. My spirit watched you, and from your own lips he learned the secret of the bane and of the antidote. Hafela mixed the poison as you taught him; I gave the remedy, and saved the king alive."

Now the knees of Hokosa grew weak beneath him, and he leaned against the fence of the kraal for support.

"I have skill in the art," he said hoarsely; "but, Messenger, your magic is more than mine, and my life is forfeit to you. To-morrow morning, you will tell the king all, and to-morrow night I shall hang upon the dreadful Tree. Well, so be it; I am overmatched at my own trade, and it is best that I should die. You have plotted well and you have conquered, and to you belong my place and power."

"It was you who plotted, and not I, Hokosa. Did you not contrive that I should reach the Great Place but a little before the poison was given to the king, so that upon me might be laid the crime of his bewitching? Did you not plan also that I should be called upon to cure him—a thing you deemed impossible—and when I failed that I should be straightway butchered?"

"Seeing that it is useless to lie to you, I confess that it was so," answered Hokosa boldly.

"It was so," repeated Owen; "therefore, according to your law your life is forfeit, seeing that you dug a pit to snare the innocent feet. But I come to tell you of a new law, and that which I preach I practise. Hokosa, I pardon you, and if you will put aside your evil-doing, I promise you that no word of all your wickedness shall pass my lips."

"It has not been my fashion to take a boon at the hand of any man, save of the king only," said the wizard in a humble voice; "but now it seems that I am come to this. Tell me, White Man, what is the payment that you seek of me?"

"None, Hokosa, except that you cease from evil and listen with an open heart to that message which I am sworn to deliver to you and to all your nation. Also you would do well to put away that fair woman whose price was the murder of him that fed you."

"I cannot do it," answered the wizard. "I will listen to your teaching, but I will not rob my heart of her it craves alone. White Man, I am not like the rest of my nation. I have not sought after women; I have but one wife, and she is old and childless. Now, for the first time in my days, I love this girl—ah, you know not how!—and I will take her, and she shall be the mother of my children."

"Then, Hokosa, you will take her to your sorrow," answered Owen solemnly, "for she will learn to hate you who have robbed her of royalty and rule, giving her wizardries and your grey hairs in place of them."

And thus for that night they parted.

CHAPTER VIII

THE FIRST TRIAL BY FIRE

On the following day, while Owen sat eating his morning meal with a thankful heart, a messenger arrived saying that the king would receive him whenever it pleased him to come. He answered that he would be with him before noon, for already he had learned that among natives one loses little by delay. A great man, they think, is rich in time, and hurries only to wait upon his superiors.

At the appointed hour a guard came to lead him to the royal house, and thither Owen went, followed by John bearing a Bible. Umsuka was seated beneath a reed roof supported by poles and open on all sides; behind him stood councillors and attendants, and by him were Nodwengo the prince, and Hokosa, his mouth and prophet. Although the day was hot, he wore a kaross or rug of wild catskins, and his face showed that the effects of the poisoned draught were still upon him. At the approach of Owen he rose with something of an effort, and, shaking him by the hand, thanked him for his life, calling him "doctor of doctors."

"Tell me, Messenger," he added, "how it was that you were able to cure me, and who were in the plot to kill me? There must have been more than one," and he rolled his eyes round with angry suspicion.

"King," answered Owen, "if I knew anything of this matter, the Power that wrote it on my mind has wiped it out again, or, at the least, has forbidden me to speak of its secret. I saved you, it is enough; for the rest, the past is the past, and I come to deal with the present and the future."

"This white man keeps his word," thought Hokosa to himself, and he looked at him thanking him with his eyes.

"So be it," answered the king; "after all, it is wise not to stir a dung-heap, for there we find little beside evil odours and the nests of snakes. Now, what is your business with me, and why do you come from the white man's countries to visit me? I have heard of those countries, they are great and far away. I have heard of the white men also—wonderful men who have all knowledge; but I do not desire to have anything to do with them, for whenever they meet black people they eat them up, taking their lands and making them slaves. Once, some years ago, two of you white people visited us here, but perhaps you know that story."

"I know it," answered Owen; "one of those men you murdered, and the other you sent back with a message which he delivered into my ears across the waters; thousands of miles away."

"Nay," answered the king, "we did not murder him; he came to us with the story of a new God who could raise the dead and work other miracles, and gave such powers to His servants. So a man was slain and we begged of him to bring him back to life; and since he could not, we killed him also because he was a liar."

"He was no liar," said Owen; "since he never told you that he had power to open the mouth of the grave. Still, Heaven is merciful, and although you murdered him that was sent to you, his Master has chosen me to follow in his footsteps. Me also you may murder if you will, and then another and another; but still the messengers shall come, till at last your ears are opened and you listen. Only, for such deeds your punishment must be heavy."

"What is the message, White Man?"

"A message of peace, of forgiveness, and of life beyond the grave, of life everlasting. Listen, King. Yesterday you were near to death; say now, had you stepped over the edge of it, where would you be this day?"

Umsuka shrugged his shoulders. "With my fathers, White Man."

"And where are your fathers?"

"Nay, I know not—nowhere, everywhere: the night is full of them; in the night we hear the echo of their voices. When they are angry they haunt the thunder-cloud, and when they are pleased they smile in the sunshine. Sometimes also they appear in the shape of snakes, or visit us in dreams, and then we offer them sacrifice. Yonder on the hillside is a haunted wood; it is full of their spirits, White Man, but they cannot talk, they only mutter, and their footfalls sound like the dropping of heavy rain, for they are strengthless and unhappy, and in the end they fade away."

"So you say," answered Owen, "who are not altogether without understanding, yet know little, never having been taught. Now listen to me," and very earnestly he preached to him and those about him of peace, of forgiveness, and of life everlasting.

"Why should a God die miserably upon a cross?" asked the king at length.

"That through His sacrifice men might become as gods," answered Owen. "Believe in Him and He will save you."

"How can we do that," asked the king again, "when already we have a god? Can we desert one god and set up another?"

"What god, King?"

"I will show him to you, White Man. Let my litter be brought."

The litter was brought and the king entered it with labouring breath. Passing through the north gate of the Great Place, the party ascended a slope of the hill that lay beyond it till they reached a flat plain some hundreds of yards in width. On this plain vegetation grew scantily, for here the bed rock of ironstone, denuded with frequent and heavy rains, was scarcely hidden by a thin crust of earth. On the further side of the plain, however, and separated from it by a little stream, was a green bank of deep soft soil, beyond which lay a gloomy valley full of great trees, that for many generations had been the burying-place of the kings of the Amasuka.

"This is the house of the god," said the king.

"A strange house," answered Owen, "and where is he that dwells in it?"

"Follow me and I will show you, Messenger; but be swift, for already the sky grows dark with coming tempest."

Now at the king's command the bearers bore him across the sere plateau towards a stone that lay almost in its centre. Presently they halted, and, pointing to this mass, the king said:—

"Behold the god!"

Owen advanced and examined the object. A glance told him that this god of the Amasuka was a meteoric stone of unusual size. Most of such stones are mere shapeless lumps, but this one bore a peculiar resemblance to a seated human being holding up one arm towards the sky. So strange was this likeness that, other reasons apart, it seemed not wonderful that savages should regard the thing with awe and veneration. Rather would it have been wonderful had they not done so.

"Say now," said Owen to the king when he had inspected the stone, "what is the history of this dumb god of yours, and why do you worship him?"

"Follow me across the stream and I will tell you, Messenger," answered the king, again glancing at the sky. "The storm gathers, and when it breaks none are safe upon this plain except the heaven doctors such as Hokosa and his companions who can bind the lightning."

So they went and when they reached the further side of the stream Umsuka descended from his litter.

"Messenger," he said, "this is the story of the god as it has come down to us. From the beginning our land has been scourged with lightning above all other lands, and with the floods of rain that accompany the lightning. In the old days the Great Place of the king was out yonder among the mountains, but every year fire from heaven fell upon it, destroying much people: and at length in a great tempest the house of the king of that day was smitten and burned, and his wives and children were turned to ashes. Then that king held a council of his wizards and fire-doctors, and these having consulted the spirits of their forefathers, retired into a place apart to fast and pray; yes, it was in yonder valley, the burying ground of kings, that they hid themselves. Now on the third night the God of Fire appeared to the chief of the doctors in his sleep, and he was shaped like a burning brand and smoke went up from him. Out of the smoke he spoke to the doctor, saying: 'For this reason it is that I torment your people, that they hate me and curse at me and pay me little honour.'

"In his dream the doctor answered: 'How can the people honour a god that they do not see?' Then the god said: 'Rise up now in the night, all the company of you, and go take your stand upon the banks of yonder stream, and I will fall down in fire from heaven, and there on the plain you shall find my image. Then let your king move his Great Place into the valley beneath the plain, and henceforth my bolts shall spare it and him. Only, month by month you shall make prayers and offerings to me; moreover, the name of the people shall be changed, for it shall be called the People of Fire.'

"Now the doctor rose, and having awakened his companions, he told them of his vision. Then they all of them went down to the banks of this stream where we now stand. And as they waited there a great tempest burst over them, and in the midst of that tempest they saw the flaming figure of a man descend from heaven, and when he touched the earth it shook. The morning came and there upon the plain before them, where there had been nothing, sat the likeness of the god as it sits to-day and shall sit for ever. So the name of this people was changed, and the king's Great Place was built where it now is.

"Since that day, Messenger, no hut has been burned and no man killed in or about the Great Place by fire from heaven, which falls only here where the god is, though away among the mountains and elsewhere men are sometimes killed. But wait a while and you shall see with your eyes. Hokosa, do you, whom the lightning will not touch, take that pole of dead wood and set it up yonder in the crevice of the rock not far from the figure of the god."

"I obey," said Hokosa, "although I have brought no medicines with me. Perhaps," he added with a faint sneer, "the white man, who is so great a wizard, will not be afraid to accompany me."

Now Owen saw that all those present were looking at him curiously. It was evident they believed that he would not dare to accept the challenge. Therefore he answered at once and without hesitation:—

"Certainly I will come; the pole is heavy for one man to carry, and where Hokosa goes, there I can go also."

"Nay, nay, Messenger," said the king, "the lightning knows Hokosa and will turn from him, but you are a stranger to it and it will eat you up."

"King," answered Owen, "I do not believe that Hokosa has any power over the lightning. It may strike him or it may strike me; but unless my God so commands, it will strike neither of us."

"On your head be it, White Man," said Hokosa, with cold anger. "Come, aid me with the pole."

Then they lifted the dead tree, and between them carried it into the middle of the plain, where they set it up in a crevice of the rock. By this time the storm was almost over them, and watching it Owen perceived that the lightnings struck always along the bank of the stream, doubtless following a hidden line of the bed of ironstone.

"It is but a very little storm," said Hokosa contemptuously, "such as visit us almost every afternoon at this period of the year. Ah! White Man, I would that you could see one of our great tempests, for these are worth beholding. This I fear, however, that you will never do, seeing it is likely that within some few minutes you will have passed back to that King who sent you here, with a hole in your head and a black mark down your spine."

"That we shall learn presently, Hokosa," answered Owen; "for my part, I pray that no such fate may overtake you."

Now Hokosa moved himself away, muttering and pointing with his fingers, but Owen remained standing within about thirty yards of the pole. Suddenly there came a glare of light, and the pole was split into fragments; but although the shock was perceptible, they remained unhurt. Almost immediately a second flash leaped from the cloud, and Owen saw Hokosa stagger and fall to his knees. "The man is struck," he thought to himself, but it was not so, for recovering his balance, the wizard walked back to the stream.

Owen never stirred. From boyhood courage had been one of his good qualities, but it was a courage of the spirit rather than of the flesh. For instance, at this very moment, so far as his body was concerned, he was much afraid, and did not in the least enjoy standing upon an ironstone plateau at the imminent risk of being destroyed by lightning. But even if he had not had an end to gain, he would have scorned to give way to his human frailties; also, now as always, his faith supported him. As it happened the storm, which was slight, passed by, and no more flashes fell. When it was over he walked back to where the king and his court were standing.

"Messenger," said Umsuka, "you are not only a great doctor, you are also a brave man, and such I honour. There is no one among us here, not being a lord of the lightning, who would have dared to stand upon that place with Hokosa while the flashes fell about him. Yet you have done it; it was Hokosa who was driven away. You have passed the trial by fire, and henceforth, whether we refuse your message or accept it, you are great in this land."

"There is no need to praise me, King," answered Owen. "The risk is something; but I knew that I was protected from it, seeing that I shall not die until my hour comes, and it is not yet. Listen now: your god yonder is nothing but a stone such as I have often seen before, for sometimes in great tempests they come to earth from the clouds. You are not the first people that have worshipped such a stone, but now we know better. Also this plain before you is full of iron, and iron draws the lightning. That is why it never strikes your town below. The iron attracts it more strongly than earth and huts of straw. Again, while the pole stood I was in little danger, for the lightning strikes the highest thing; but after the pole was shattered and Hokosa wisely went away, then I was in some danger, only no flashes fell. I am not a magician, King, but I know some things that you do not know, and I trust in One whom I shall lead you to trust also."

"We will talk of this more hereafter," said the king hurriedly, "for one day, I have heard and seen enough. Also I do not believe your words, for I have noted ever that those who are the greatest wizards of all say continually that they have no magic power. Hokosa, you have been famous in your day, but it seems that henceforth you who have led must follow."

"The battle is not yet fought, King," answered Hokosa. "To-day I met the lightnings without my medicines, and it was a little storm; when I am prepared with my medicines and the tempest is great, then I will challenge this white man to face me yonder, and then in that hour my god shall show his strength and his God shall not be able to save him."

"That we shall see when the time comes," answered Owen, with a smile.

That night as Owen sat in his hut working at the translation of St. John, the door was opened and Hokosa entered.

"White Man," said the wizard, "you are too strong for me, though whence you have your power I know not. Let us make a bargain. Show me your magic and I will show you mine, and we will rule the land between us. You and I are much akin—we are great; we have the spirit sight; we know that there are things beyond the things we see and hear and feel; whereas, for the rest, they are fools, following the flesh alone. I have spoken."

"Very gladly will I show you my magic, Hokosa," answered Owen cheerfully, "since, to speak truth, though I know you to be wicked, and guess that you would be glad to be rid of me by fair means or foul; yet I have taken a liking for you, seeing in you one who from a sinner may grow into a saint.

"This then is my magic: To love God and serve man; to eschew wizardry, wealth, and power; to seek after holiness, poverty and humility; to deny your flesh, and to make yourself small in the sight of men, that so perchance you may grow great in the sight of Heaven and save your soul alive."

"I have no stomach for that lesson," said Hokosa.

"Yet you shall live to hunger for it," answered Owen. And the wizard went away angered but wondering.

Now, day by day for something over a month Owen preached the Gospel before the king, his councillors, and hundreds of the head men of the nation. They listened to him attentively, debating the new doctrine point by point; for although they might be savages, these people were very keen-witted and subtle. Very patiently did Owen sow, and at length to his infinite joy he also gathered in his first-fruit. One night as he sat in his hut labouring as usual at the work of translation, wherein he was assisted by John whom he had taught to read and write, the Prince Nodwengo entered and greeted him. For a while he sat silent watching the white man at his task, then he said:—

"Messenger, I have a boon to ask of you. Can you teach me to understand those signs which you set upon the paper, and to make them also as does John your servant?"

"Certainly," answered Owen; "if you will come to me at noon to-morrow, we will begin."

The prince thanked him, but he did not go away. Indeed, from his manner Owen guessed that he had something more upon his mind. At length it came out.

"Messenger," he said, "you have told us of baptism whereby we are admitted into the army of your King; say, have you the power of this rite?"

"I have."

"And is your servant here baptised?"

"He is."

"Then if he who is a common man can be baptised, why may not I who am a prince?"

"In baptism," answered Owen, "there is no distinction between the highest and the lowest; but if you believe, then the door is open and through it you can join the company of Heaven."

"Messenger, I do believe," answered the prince humbly.

Then Owen was very joyful, and that same night, with John for a witness, he baptised the prince, giving him the new name of Constantine, after the first Christian emperor.

On the following day Nodwengo, in the presence of Owen, who on this point would suffer no concealment, announced to the king that he had become a Christian. Umsuka heard, and for a while sat silent. Then he said in a troubled voice:—

"Truly, Messenger, in the words of that Book from which you read to us, I fear that you have come hither to bring, 'not peace but a sword.' Now when the witch-doctors and the priests of fire learn this, that he whom I have chosen to succeed me has become the servant of another faith, they will stir up the soldiers and there will be civil war. I pray you, therefore, keep the matter secret, at any rate for a while, seeing that the lives of many are at stake."

"In this, my father," answered the prince, "I must do as the Messenger bids me; but if you desire it, take from me the right of succession and call back my brother from the northern mountains."

"That by poison or the spear he may put all of us to death, Nodwengo! Be not afraid; ere long when he learns all that is happening here, your brother Hafela will come from the northern mountains, and the spears of his impis shall be countless as the stars of the sky. Messenger, you desire to draw us to the arms of your God—and myself, I am at times minded to follow the path of my son Nodwengo and seek a refuge there—but say, will they be strong enough to protect us from Hafela and the warriors of the north? Already he gathers his clans, and already my captains desert to him. By-and-by, in the spring-time—may I be dead before the day—he will roll down upon us like a flood of water—"

"To fall back like waters from a wall of rock," answered Owen. "'Let not your heart be troubled,' for my Master can protect His servants, and He will protect you. But first you must confess Him openly, as your son has done."

"Nay, I am too old to hurry," said the king with a sigh. "Your tale seems full of promise to one who is near the grave; but how can I know that it is more than a dream? And shall I abandon the worship of my fathers and change, or strive to change, the customs of my people to follow after dreams? Nodwengo has chosen his part, and I do not blame him; yet, for the present I beseech you both to keep silence on this matter, lest to save bloodshed I should be driven to side against you."

"So be it, King," said Owen; "but I warn you that Truth has a loud voice, and that it is hard to hide the shining of a light in a dark place, nor does it please my Lord to be denied by those who confess Him."

"I am weary," replied the old king, and they saluted him and went.

In obedience to the wish of Umsuka his father, the conversion of Nodwengo was kept secret, and yet—none knew how—the thing leaked out. Soon the women in their huts, and the soldiers by their watch-fires, whispered it in each other's ears that he who was appointed to be their future ruler had become a servant of the unknown God. That he had forsworn war and all the delights of men; that he would take but one wife and appear before the army, not in the uniform of a general, but clad in a white robe, and carry, not the broad spear, but a cross of wood. Swiftly the strange story flew from mouth to mouth, yet it was not altogether believed till it chanced that one day when he was reviewing a regiment, a soldier who was drunk with beer openly insulted the prince, calling him "a coward who worshipped a coward."

Now men held their breaths, waiting to see this fool led away to die by torture of the ant-heap or some other dreadful doom. But the prince only answered:

"Soldier, you are drunk, therefore I forgive you your words. Whether He Whom you blaspheme will forgive you, I know not. Get you gone!"

The warriors stared and murmured, for by those words, wittingly or unwittingly, their general had confessed his faith, and that day they made ribald songs about him in the camp. But on the morrow when they learned how that the man whom the prince spared had been seized by a lion and taken away as he sat at night with his companions in the bivouac, his mouth full of boasting of his own courage in offering insult to the prince and the new faith, then they looked at each other askance and said little more of the matter. Doubtless it was chance, and yet this Spirit Whom the Messenger preached was one of Whom it seemed wisest not to speak lightly.

But still the trouble grew, for by now the witch-doctors, with Hokosa at the head of them, were frightened for their place and power, and fomented it both openly and in secret. Of the women they asked what would become of them when men were allowed to take but one wife? Of the heads of kraals, how they would grow wealthy when their daughters ceased to be worth cattle? Of the councillors and generals, how the land could be protected from its foes when they were commanded to lay down the spear? Of the soldiers, whose only trade was war, how it would please them to till the fields like girls? Dismay took hold of the nation, and although they were much loved, there was open talk of killing or driving away the king and Nodwengo who favoured the white man, and of setting up Hafela in their place.

At length the crisis came, and in this fashion. The Amasuka, like many other African tribes, had a strange veneration for certain varieties of snakes which they declared to be possessed by the spirits of their ancestors. It was a law among them that if one of these snakes entered a kraal it must not be killed, or even driven away, under pain of death, but must be allowed to share with the human occupants any hut that it might select. As a result of this enforced hospitality deaths from snake-bite were numerous among the people; but when they happened in a kraal its owners met with little sympathy, for the doctors explained that the real cause of them was the anger of some ancestral spirit towards his descendants. Now, before John was despatched to instruct Owen in the language of the Amasuka a certain girl was sealed to him as his future wife, and this girl, who during his absence had been orphaned, he had married recently with the approval of Owen, who at this time was preparing her for baptism. On the third morning after his marriage John appeared before his master in the last extremity of grief and terror.

"Help me, Messenger!" he cried, "for my ancestral spirit has entered our hut and bitten my wife as she lay asleep."

"Are you mad?" asked Owen. "What is an ancestral spirit, and how can it have bitten your wife?"

"A snake," gasped John, "a green snake of the worst sort."

Then Owen remembered the superstition, and snatching blue-stone and spirits of wine from his medicine chest, he rushed to John's hut. As it happened, he was fortunately in time with his remedies and succeeded in saving the woman's life, whereby his reputation as a doctor and a magician, already great, was considerably enlarged.

"Where is the snake?" he asked when at length she was out of danger.

"Yonder, under the kaross," answered John, pointing to a skin rug which lay in the corner.

"Have you killed it?"

"No, Messenger," answered the man, "I dare not. Alas! we must live with the thing here in the hut till it chooses to go away."

"Truly," said Owen, "I am ashamed to think that you who are a Christian should still believe so horrible a superstition. Does your faith teach you that the souls of men enter into snakes?"

Now John hung his head; then snatching a kerry, he threw aside the kaross, revealing a great green serpent seven or eight feet long. With fury he fell upon the reptile, killed it by repeated blows, and hurled it into the courtyard outside the house.

"Behold, father," he said, "and judge whether I am still superstitious." Then his countenance fell and he added: "Yet my life must pay for this deed, for it is an ancient law among us that to harm one of these snakes is death."

"Have no fear," said Owen, "a way will be found out of this trouble."

That afternoon Owen heard a great hubbub outside his kraal, and going to see what was the matter, he found a party of the witch-doctors dragging John towards the place of judgment, which was by the king's house. Thither he followed to discover that the case was already in course of being opened before the king, his council, and a vast audience of the people. Hokosa was the accuser. In brief and pregnant sentences, producing the dead snake in proof of his argument, he pointed out the enormity of the offence against the laws of the Amasuka wherewith the prisoner was charged, demanding that the man who had killed the house of his ancestral spirit should instantly be put to death.

"What have you to say?" asked the king of John.

"This, O King," replied John, "that I am a Christian, and to me that snake is nothing but a noxious reptile. It bit my wife, and had it not been for the medicine of the Messenger, she would have perished of the poison. Therefore I killed it before it could harm others."

"It is a fair answer," said the king. "Hokosa, I think that this man should go free."

"The king's will is the law," replied Hokosa bitterly; "but if the law were the king's will, the decision would be otherwise. This man has slain, not a snake, but that which held the spirit of an ancestor, and for the deed he deserves to die. Hearken, O King, for the business is larger than it seems. How are we to be governed henceforth? Are we to follow our ancient rules and customs, or must we submit ourselves to a new rule and a new custom? I tell you, O King, that the people murmur; they are without light, they wander in the darkness, they cannot understand. Play with us no more, but let us hear the truth that we may judge of this matter."

Umsuka looked at Owen, but made no reply.

"I will answer you, Hokosa," said Owen, "for I am the spring of all this trouble, and at my command that man, my disciple, killed yonder snake. What is it? It is nothing but a reptile; no human spirit ever dwelt within it as you imagine in your superstition. You ask to hear the truth; day by day I have preached it in your ears and you have not listened, though many among you have listened and understood. What is it that you seek?"

"We seek, Messenger, to be rid of you, your fantasies and your religion; and we demand that our king should expel you and restore the ancient laws, or failing this, that you should prove your power openly before us all. Your word, O King!"

Umsuka thought for a while and answered:—

"This is my word, Hokosa: I will not drive the Messenger from the land, for he is a good man; he saved my life, and there is virtue in his teaching, towards which I myself incline. Yet it is just that he should be asked to prove his power, so that an end may be put to doubt and all of us may learn what god we are to worship."

"How can I prove my power," asked Owen, "further than I have proved it already? Does Hokosa desire to set up his god against my God—the false against the true?"

"I do," answered the wizard with passion, "and according to the issue let the judgment be. Let us halt no longer between two opinions, let us become wholly Christian or rest wholly heathen, for to be divided is to be destroyed. The magic of the Messenger is great; once and for all let us learn if it is more than our magic. Let us put him and his doctrines to the trial by fire."

"What is the trial by fire?" asked Owen.

"You have seen something of it, White Man, but not much. This is the trial by fire: to stand yonder before the face of the god of thunder when a great tempest rages—not such a storm as you saw, but a storm that splits the heavens—and to come thence unscathed. Listen: I who am a 'heaven-herd,' I who know the signs of the weather, tell you that within two days such a tempest as this will break upon us. Then White Man, I and my companions will be ready to meet you on the plain. Take the cross by which you swear and set it up yonder and stand by it, and with you your converts, Nodwengo the prince, and this man whom you have named John, if they dare to go. Over against you, around the symbol of the god by which we swear, will stand I and my company, and we will pray our god and you shall pray your God. Then the storm will break upon us, and when it is ended we shall learn which of us remain alive. If you and your cross are shattered, to us will be the victory; if we are laid low, take it for your own. Your judgment, King!"

Again Umsuka thought and answered:—

"So be it. Messenger, hear me. There is no need for you to accept this challenge; but if you will not accept it, then go from my country in peace, taking with you those who cleave to you. If on the other hand you do accept it, these shall be the stakes: that if you pass the trial unharmed, and the fire-doctors are swept away, your creed shall be my creed and the creed of the land; but if the fire-doctors prevail against you, then it shall be death or banishment to any who profess that creed. Now choose!"

"I have chosen," said Owen. "I will meet Hokosa and his company on the Place of fire whenever he may appoint, but for the others I cannot say."

"We will come with you," said Nodwengo and John, with one voice; "where you go, Messenger, we will surely follow."

CHAPTER X

THE SECOND TRIAL BY FIRE

When this momentous discussion was finished, as usual Owen preached before the king, expounding the Scriptures and taking for his subject the duty of faith. As he went back to his hut he saw that the snake which John had killed had been set upon a pole in that part of the Great Place which served as a market, and that hundreds of natives were gathered beneath it gesticulating and talking excitedly.

"See the work of Hokosa," he thought to himself. "Moses set up a serpent to save the people; yonder wizard sets up one to destroy them."

That evening Owen had no heart for his labours, for his mind was heavy at the prospect of the trial which lay before him. Not that he cared for his own life, for of this he scarcely thought; it was the prospects of his cause which troubled him. It seemed much to expect that Heaven again should throw over him the mantle of its especial protection, and yet if it did not do so there was an end of his mission among the People of Fire. Well, he did not seek this trial—he would have avoided it if he could, but it had been thrust upon him, and he was forced to choose between it and the abandonment of the work which he had undertaken with such high hopes and pushed so far toward success. He did not choose the path, it had been pointed out to him to walk upon; and if it ended in a precipice, at least he would have done his best.

As he thought thus John entered the hut, panting.

"What is the matter?" Owen asked.

"Father, the people saw and pursued me because of the death of that accursed snake. Had I not run fast and escaped them, I think they would have killed me."

"At least you have escaped, John; so be comforted and return thanks."

"Father," said the man presently, "I know that you are great, and can do many wonderful things, but have you in truth power over lightning?"

"Why do you ask?"

"Because a great tempest is brewing, and if you have not we shall certainly be killed when we stand yonder on the Place of Fire."

"John," he said, "I cannot speak to the lightning in a voice which it can hear. I cannot say to it 'go yonder,' or 'come hither,' but He Who made it can do so. Why do you tempt me with your doubts? Have I not told you the story of Elijah the prophet and the priests of Baal? Did Elijah's Master forsake him, and shall He forsake us? Also this is certain, that all the medicine of Hokosa and his wizards will not turn a lightning flash by the breadth of a single hair. God alone can turn it, and for the sake of His cause among these people I believe that He will do so."

Thus Owen spoke on till, in reproving the weakness of another, he felt his own faith come back to him and, remembering the past and how he had been preserved in it, the doubt and trouble went out of his mind to return no more.

The third day—the day of trial—came. For sixty hours or more the heat of the weather had been intense; indeed, during all that time the thermometer in Owen's hut, notwithstanding the protection of a thick hatch, had shown the temperature to vary between a maximum of 113 and a minimum of 101 degrees. Now, in the early morning, it stood at 108.

"Will the storm break to-day?" asked Owen of Nodwengo, who came to visit him.

"They say so, Messenger, and I think it by the feel of the air. If so, it will be a very great storm, for the heaven is full of fire. Already Hokosa and the doctors are at their rites upon the plain yonder, but there will be no need to join them till two hours after midday."

"Is the cross ready?" asked Owen.

"Yes, and set up. It is a heavy cross; six men could scarcely carry it. Oh! Messenger, I am not afraid—and yet, have you no medicine? If not, I fear that the lightning will fall upon the cross as it fell upon the pole and then—"

"Listen, Nodwengo," said Owen, "I know a medicine, but I will not use it. You see that waggon chain? Were one end of it buried in the ground and the other with a spear blade made fast to it hung to the top of the cross, we could live out the fiercest storm in safety. But I say that I will not use it. Are we witch doctors that we should take refuge in tricks? No, let faith be our shield, and if it fail us, then let us die. Pray now with me that it may not fail us."

It was afternoon. All round the Field of Fire were gathered thousands upon thousands of the people of the Amasuka. The news of this duel between the God of the white man and their god had travelled far and wide, and even the very aged who could scarcely crawl and the little ones who must be carried were collected there to see the issue. Nor had they need to fear disappointment, for already the sky was half hidden by dense thunder-clouds piled ridge on ridge, and the hush of the coming tempest lay upon the earth. Round about the meteor stone which they called a god, each of them stirring a little gourd of medicine that was placed upon the ground before him, but uttering no word, were gathered Hokosa and his followers to the number of twenty. They were all of them arrayed in their snakeskin dresses and other wizard finery. Also each man held in his hand a wand fashioned from a human thigh-bone. In front of the stone burned a little fire, which now and again Hokosa fed with aromatic leaves, at the same time pouring medicine from his bowl upon the holy stone. Opposite the symbol of the god, but at a good distance from it, a great cross of white wood was set up in the rock by a spot which the witch-doctors themselves had chosen. Upon the banks of the stream, in the place apart, were the king, his councillors and the regiment on guard, and with them Owen, the Prince Nodwengo and John.

"The storm will be fierce," said the king uneasily, glancing at the western sky, upon whose bosom the blue lightnings played with an incessant flicker. Then he bade those about him stand back, and calling Owen and the prince to him, said: "Messenger, my son tells me that your wisdom knows a plan whereby you may be preserved from the fury of the tempest. Use it, I pray of you, Messenger, that your life may be saved, and with it the life of the only son who is left to me."

"I cannot," answered Owen, "for thus by doubting Him I should tempt my Master. Still, it is not laid upon the prince to accompany through this trial. Let him stay here, and I alone will stand beneath the cross."

"Stay, Nodwengo," implored the old man.

"I did not think to live to hear my father bid me, one of the royal blood of the Amasuka, to desert my captain in the hour of battle and hide myself in the grass like a woman," answered the prince with a bitter smile. "Nay, it may be that death awaits me yonder, but nothing except death shall keep me back from the venture."

"It is well spoken," said the king; "be it as you will."

Now the company of wizards, leaving their medicine-pots upon the ground, formed themselves in a treble line, and marching to where the king stood, they saluted him. Then they sang the praises of their god, and in a song that had been prepared, heaped insult upon the God of the white man and upon the messenger who preached Him. To all of this Owen listened in silence.

"He is a coward!" cried their spokesman; "he has not a word to say. He skulks there in his white robes behind the majesty of the king. Let him go forth and stand by his piece of wood. He dare not go! He thinks the hillside safer. Come out, little White Man, and we will show you how we manage the lightnings. Ah! they shall fly about you like spears in battle. You shall throw yourself upon the ground and shriek in terror, and then they will lick you up and you shall be no more, and there will be an end of you and the symbol of your God."

"Cease your boastings," said the king shortly, "and get you back to your place, knowing that if it should chance that the white man conquers you will be called upon to answer for these words."

"We shall be ready, O King," they cried; and amidst the cheers of the vast audience they marched back to their station, still singing the blasphemous mocking song.

Now to the west all the heavens were black as night, though the eastern sky still showed blue and cloudless. Nature lay oppressed with silence—silence intense and unnatural; and so great was the heat that the air danced visibly above the ironstone as it dances about a glowing stove. Suddenly the quietude was broken by a moaning sound of wind; the grass stirred, the leaves of the trees began to shiver, and an icy breath beat upon Owen's brow.

"Let us be going," he said, and lifting the ivory crucifix above his head, he passed the stream and walked towards the wooden cross. After him came the Prince Nodwengo, wearing his royal dress of leopard skin, and after him, John, arrayed in a linen robe.

As the little procession appeared to their view some of the soldiers began to mock, but almost instantly the laughter died away. Rude as they were, these savages understood that here was no occasion for their mirth, that the three men indeed seemed clothed with a curious dignity. Perhaps it was their slow and quiet gait, perhaps a sense of the errand upon which they were bound; or it may have been the strange unearthly light that fell upon them from over the edge of the storm cloud; at the least, as the multitude became aware, their appearance was impressive. They reached the cross and took up their stations there, Owen in front of it, Nodwengo to the right, and John to the left.

Now a sharp squall of strong wind swept across the space, and with it came a flaw of rain. It passed by, and the storm that had been muttering and growling in the distance began to burst. The great clouds seemed to grow and swell, and from the breast of them swift lightnings leapt, to be met by other lightnings rushing upwards from the earth. The air was filled with a tumult of uncertain wind and a hiss as of distant rain. Then the batteries of thunder were opened, and the world shook with their volume. Down from on high the flashes fell blinding and incessant, and by the light of them the fire-doctors could be seen running to and fro, pointing now here and now there with their wands of human bones, and pouring the medicines from their gourds upon the ground and upon each other. Owen and his two companions could be seen also, standing quietly with clasped hands, while above them towered the tall white cross.

At length the storm was straight over head. Slowly it advanced in its awe-inspiring might as flash after flash, each more fantastic and horrible than the last, smote upon the floor of ironstone. It played about the shapes of the doctors, who in the midst of it looked like devils in an inferno. It crept onwards towards the station of the cross, but—it never reached the cross.

One flash struck indeed within fifty paces of where Owen stood. Then of a sudden a marvel happened, or something which to this day the People of Fire talk of as a marvel, for in an instant the rain began to pour like a wall of water stretching from earth to heaven, and the wind changed. It had been blowing from the west, now it blew from the east with the force of a gale.

It blew and rolled the tempest back upon itself, causing it to return to the regions whence it had gathered. At the very foot of the cross its march was stayed; there was the water-line, as straight as if it had been drawn with a rule. The thunder-clouds that were pressed forward met the clouds that were pressed back, and together they seemed to come to earth, filling the air with a gloom so dense that the eye could not pierce it. To the west was a wall of blackness towering to the heavens; to the east, light, blue and unholy, gleamed upon the white cross and the figures of its watchers.

For some seconds—twenty or more—there was a lull, and then it seemed as though all hell had broken loose upon the world. The wall of blackness became a wall of flame, in which strange and ardent shapes appeared ascending and descending; the thunder bellowed till the mountains rocked, and in one last blaze, awful and indescribable, the skies melted into a deluge of fire. In the flare of it Owen thought that he saw the figures of men falling this way and that, then he staggered against the cross for support and his senses failed him.

When they returned again, he perceived the storm being drawn back from the face of the pale earth like a pall from the face of the dead, and he heard a murmur of fear and wonder rising from ten thousand throats.

Well might they fear and wonder, for of the twenty and one wizards eleven were dead, four were paralysed by shock, five were flying in their terror, and one, Hokosa himself, stood staring at the fallen, a very picture of despair. Nor was this all, for the meteor stone with a human shape which for generations the People of Fire had worshipped as a god, lay upon the plain in fused and shattered fragments.

The people saw, and a sound as of a hollow groan of terror went up from them. Then they were silent. For a while Owen and his companions were silent also, since their hearts were too full for speech. Then he said:—

"As the snake fell harmless from the hand of Paul, so has the lightning turned back from me, who strive to follow in his footsteps, working death and dismay among those who would have harmed us. May forgiveness be theirs who were without understanding. Brethren, let us return and make report to the king."

Now, as they had come, so they went back; first Owen with the crucifix, next to him Nodwengo, and last of the three John. They drew near to the king, when suddenly, moved by a common impulse, the thousands of the people upon the banks of the stream with one accord threw themselves upon their knees before Owen, calling him God and offering him worship. Infected by the contagion, Umsuka, his guard and his councillors followed their example, so that of all the multitude Hokosa alone remained upon his feet, standing by his dishonoured and riven deity.

"Rise!" cried Owen aghast. "Would you do sacrilege, and offer worship to a man? Rise, I command you!"

Then the king rose, saying:—

"You are no man, Messenger, you are a spirit."

"He is a spirit," repeated the multitude after him.

"I am not a spirit, I am yet a man," cried Owen again, "but the Spirit Whom I serve has made His power manifest in me His servant, and your idols are smitten with the sword of His power, O ye Sons of Fire! Hokosa still lives, let him be brought hither."

They fetched Hokosa, and he stood before them.

"You have seen, Wizard," said the king. "What have you to say?"

"Nothing," answered Hokosa, "save that victory is to the Cross, and to the white man who preaches it, for his magic is greater than our magic. By his command the tempest was stayed, and the boasts we hurled fell back upon our heads and the head of our god to destroy us."

"Yes," said the king, "victory is to the Cross, and henceforth the Cross shall be worshipped in this land, or at least no other god shall be worshipped. Let us be going. Come with me, Messenger, Lord of the Lightning."

CHAPTER XI

On the morrow Owen baptised the king, many of his councillors, and some twenty others whom he considered fit to receive the rite. Also he despatched his first convert John, with other messengers, on a three months' journey to the coast, giving them letters acquainting the bishop and others with his marvellous success, and praying that missionaries might be sent to assist him in his labours.

Now day by day the Church grew till it numbered hundreds of souls, and thousands more hovered on its threshold. From dawn to dark Owen toiled, preaching, exhorting, confessing, gathering in his harvest; and from dark to midnight he pored over his translation of the Scriptures, teaching Nodwengo and a few others how to read and write them. But although his efforts were crowned with so signal and extraordinary a triumph, he was well aware of the dangers that threatened the life of the infant Church. Many accepted it indeed, and still more tolerated it; but there remained multitudes who regarded the new religion with suspicion and veiled hatred. Nor was this strange, seeing that the hearts of men are not changed in an hour or their ancient customs easily overset.

On one point, indeed, Owen had to give way. The Amasuka were a polygamous people; all their law and traditions were interwoven with polygamy, and to abolish that institution suddenly and with violence would have brought their social fabric to the ground. Now, as he knew well, the missionary Church declares in effect that no man can be both a Christian and a polygamist; therefore among the followers of that custom the missionary Church makes but little progress. Not without many qualms and hesitations, Owen, having only the Scriptures to consult, came to a compromise with his converts. If a man already married to more than one wife wished to become a Christian, he permitted him to do so upon the condition that he took no more wives; while a man unmarried at the time of his conversion might take one wife only. This decree, liberal as it was, caused great dissatisfaction among both men and women. But it was as nothing compared to the feeling that was evoked by Owen's preaching against all war not undertaken in self-defence, and against the strict laws which he prevailed upon the king to pass, suppressing the practice of wizardry, and declaring the chief or doctor who caused a man to be "smelt out" and killed upon charges of witchcraft to be guilty of murder.

At first whenever Owen went abroad he was surrounded by thousands of people who followed him in the expectation that he would work miracles, which, after his exploits with the lightning, they were well persuaded that he could do if he chose. But he worked no more miracles; he only preached to them a doctrine adverse to their customs and foreign to their thoughts.

So it came about that in time, when the novelty was gone off and the story of his victory over the Fire-god had grown stale, although the work of conversion went on steadily, many of the people grew weary of the white man and his doctrines. Soon this weariness found expression in various ways, and in none more markedly than by the constant desertions from the ranks of the king's regiments. At first, by Owen's advice, the king tolerated these desertions; but at length, having obtained information that an entire regiment purposed absconding at dawn, he caused it to be surrounded and seized by night. Next morning he addressed that regiment, saying:—

"Soldiers, you think that because I have become a Christian and will not permit unnecessary bloodshed, I am also become a fool. I will teach you otherwise. One man in every twenty of you shall be killed, and henceforth any soldier who attempts to desert will be killed also!"

The order was carried out, for Owen could not find a word to say against it, with the result that desertions almost ceased, though not before the king had lost some eight or nine thousand of his best soldiers. Worst of all, these soldiers had gone to join Hafela in his mountain fastnesses; and the rumour grew that ere long they would appear again, to claim the crown for him or to take it by force of arms.

Now too a fresh complication arose. The old king sickened of his last illness, and soon it became known that he must die. A month later die he did, passing away peacefully in Owen's arms, and with his last breath exhorting his people to cling to the Christian religion; to take Nodwengo for their king and to be faithful to him.

The king died, and that same day was buried by Owen in the gloomy resting-place of the blood-royal of the People of Fire, where a Christian priest now set foot for the first time.

On the morrow Nodwengo was proclaimed king with much ceremony in face of the people and of all the army that remained to him. One captain raised a cry for Hafela his brother. Nodwengo caused him to be seized and brought before him.

"Man," he said, "on this my coronation day I will not stain my hand with blood. Listen. You cry upon Hafela, and to Hafela you shall go, taking him this message. Tell him that I, Nodwengo, have succeeded to the crown of Umsuka, my father, by his will and the will of the people. Tell him it is true that I have become a Christian, and that Christians follow not after war but peace. Tell him, however, that though I am a Christian I have not forgotten how to fight or how to rule. It has reached my ears that it is his purpose to attack me with a great force which he is gathering, and to possess himself of my throne. If he should choose to come, I shall be ready to meet him; but I counsel him against coming, for it will be to find his death. Let him stay where he is in peace, and be my subject; or let him go afar with those that cleave to him, and set up a kingdom of his own, for then I shall not follow him; but let him not dare to lift a spear against me, his sovereign, since if he does so he shall be treated as a rebel and find the doom of a rebel. Begone, and show your face here no more!"

The man crept away crestfallen; but all who heard that speech broke into cheering, which, as its purport was repeated from rank to rank, spread far and wide; for now the army learned that in becoming a Christian, Nodwengo had not become a woman. Of this indeed he soon gave them ample proof. The old king's grip upon things had been lax, that of Nodwengo was like iron. He practised no cruelties, and did injustice to none; but his discipline was severe, and soon the regiments were brought to a greater pitch of proficiency than they had ever reached before, although they were now allowed to marry when they pleased, a boon that hitherto had been denied to them. Moreover, by Owen's help, he designed an entirely new system of fortification of the kraal and surrounding hills, which would, it was thought, make the place impregnable. These and many other acts, equally vigorous and far-seeing, put new heart into the nation. Also the report of them put fear into Hafela, who, it was rumoured, had now given up all idea of attack.

Some there were, however, who looked upon these changes with little love, and Hokosa was one of them. After his defeat in the duel by fire, for a while his spirit was crushed. Hitherto he had more or less been a believer in the protecting influence of his own god or fetish, who would, as he thought, hold his priests scatheless from the lightning. Often and often had he stood in past days upon that plain while the great tempests broke around his head, and returned thence unharmed, attributing to sorcery a safety that was really due to chance. From time to time indeed a priest was killed; but, so his companions held, the misfortune resulted invariably from the man's neglect of some rite, or was a mark of the anger of the heavens.

Now Hokosa had lived to see all these convictions shattered: he had seen the lightning, which he pretended to be able to control, roll back upon him from the foot of the Christian cross, reducing his god to nothingness and his companions to corpses.

At first Hokosa was dismayed, but as time went on hope came back to him. Stripped of his offices and power, and from the greatest in the nation, after the king, become one of small account, still no harm or violence was attempted towards him. He was left wealthy and in peace, and living thus he watched and listened with open eyes and ears, waiting till the tide should turn. It seemed that he would not have long to wait, for reasons that have been told.

"Why do you sit here like a vulture on a rock," asked the girl Noma, whom he had taken to wife, "when you might be yonder with Hafela, preparing him by your wisdom for the coming war?"

"Because I am a king-vulture, and I wait for the sick bull to die," he answered, pointing to the Great Place beneath him. "Say, why should I bring Hafela to prey upon a carcase I have marked down for my own?"

"Now you speak well," said Noma; "the bull suffers from a strange disease, and when he is dead another must lead the herd."

"That is so," answered her husband, "and, therefore, I am patient."

It was shortly after this conversation that the old king died, with results very different from those which Hokosa had anticipated. Although he was a Christian, to his surprise Nodwengo showed that he was also a strong ruler, and that there was little chance of the sceptre slipping from his hand—none indeed while the white teacher was there to guide him.

"What will you do now, Hokosa?" asked Noma his wife upon a certain day. "Will you turn to Hafela after all?"

"No," answered Hokosa; "I will consult my ancient lore. Listen. Whatever else is false, this is true: that magic exists, and I am its master. For a while it seemed to me that the white man was greater at the art than I am; but of late I have watched him and listened to his doctrines, and I believe that this is not so. It is true that in the beginning he read my plans in a dream, or otherwise; it is true that he hurled the lightning back upon my head; but I hold that these things were accidents. Again and again he has told us that he is not a wizard; and if this be so, he can be overcome."

"How, husband?"

"How? By wizardry. This very night, Noma, with your help I will consult the dead, as I have done in bygone time, and learn the future from their lips which cannot lie."

"So be it; though the task is hateful to me, and I hate you who force me to it."

Noma answered thus with passion, but her eyes shone as she spoke: for those who have once tasted the cup of magic are ever drawn to drink of it again, even when they fear the draught.

It was midnight, and Hokosa with his wife stood in the burying-ground of the kings of the Amasuka. Before Owen came upon his mission it was death to visit this spot except upon the occasion of the laying to rest of one of the royal blood, or to offer the annual sacrifice to the spirits of the dead. Even beneath the bright moon that shone upon it the place seemed terrible. Here in the bosom of the hills was an amphitheatre, surrounded by walls of rock varying from five hundred to a thousand feet in height. In this amphitheatre grew great mimosa thorns, and above them towered pillars of granite, set there not by the hand of man but by nature. It would seem that the Amasuka, led by some fine instinct, had chosen these columns as fitting memorials of their kings, at the least a departed monarch lay at the foot of each of them.

The smallest of these unhewn obelisks—it was about fifty feet high—marked the resting-place of Umsuka; and deep into its granite Owen with his own hand had cut the dead king's name and date of death, surmounting his inscription with a symbol of the cross.

Towards this pillar Hokosa made his way through the wet grass, followed by Noma his wife. Presently they were there, standing one upon each side of a little mound of earth more like an ant-heap than a grave; for, after the custom of his people, Umsuka had been buried sitting. At the foot of each of the pillars rose a heap of similar shape, but many times as large. The kings who slept there were accompanied to their resting-places by numbers of their wives and servants, who had been slain in solemn sacrifice that they might attend their Lord whithersoever he should wander.

"What is that you desire and would do?" asked Noma, in a hushed voice. Bold as she was, the place and the occasion awed her.

"I desire wisdom from the dead!" he answered. "Have I not already told you, and can I not win it with your help?"

"What dead, husband?"

"Umsuka the king. Ah! I served him living, and at the last he drove me away from his side. Now he shall serve me, and out of the nowhere I will call him back to mine."

"Will not this symbol defeat you?" and Noma pointed at the cross hewn in the granite.

At her words a sudden gust of rage seemed to shake the wizard. His still eyes flashed, his lips turned livid, and with them he spat upon the cross.

"It has no power," he said. "May it be accursed, and may he who believes therein hang thereon! It has no power; but even if it had, according to the tale of that white liar, such things as I would do have been done beneath its shadow. By it the dead have been raised—ay! dead kings have been dragged from death and forced to tell the secrets of the grave. Come, come, let us to the work."

"What must I do, husband?"

"You shall sit you there, even as a corpse sits, and there for a little while you shall die—yes, your spirit shall leave you—and I will fill your body with the soul of him who sleeps beneath; and through your lips I will learn his wisdom, to whom all things are known."

"It is terrible! I am afraid!" she said. "Cannot this be done otherwise?"

"It cannot," he answered. "The spirits of the dead have no shape or form; they are invisible, and can speak only in dreams or through the lips of one in whose pulses life still lingers, though soul and body be already parted. Have no fear. Ere his ghost leaves you it shall recall your own, which till the corpse is cold stays ever close at hand. I did not think to find a coward in you, Noma."

"I am not a coward, as you know well," she answered passionately, "for many a deed of magic have we dared together in past days. But this is fearsome, to die that my body may become the home of the ghost of a dead man, who perchance, having entered it, will abide there, leaving my spirit houseless, or perchance will shut up the doors of my heart in such fashion that they never can be opened. Can it not be done by trance as aforetime? Tell me, Hokosa, how often have you thus talked with the dead?"

"Thrice, Noma."

"And what chanced to them through whom you talked?"

"Two lived and took no harm; the third died, because the awakening medicine lacked power. Yet fear nothing; that which I have with me is of the best. Noma, you know my plight: I must win wisdom or fall for ever, and you alone can help me; for under this new rule, I can no longer buy a youth or maid for purposes of witchcraft, even if one could be found fitted to the work. Choose then: shall we go back or forward? Here trance will not help us; for those entranced cannot read the future, nor can they hold communion with the dead, being but asleep. Choose, Noma."

"I have chosen," she answered. "Never yet have I turned my back upon a venture, nor will I do so now. Come life, come death, I will submit me to your wish, though there are few women who would dare as much for any man. Nor in truth do I do this for you, Hokosa; I do it because I seek power, and thus only can we win it who are fallen. Also I love all things strange, and desire to commune with the dead and to know that, if for some few minutes only, at least my woman's breast has held the spirit of a king. Yet, I warn you, make no fault in your magic; for should I die beneath it, then I, who desire to live on and to be great, will haunt you and be avenged upon you!"

"Oh! Noma," he said, "if I believed that there was any danger for you, should I ask you to suffer this thing?—I, who love you more even than you love power, more than my life, more than anything that is or ever can be."

"I know it, and it is to that I trust," the woman answered. "Now begin, before my courage leaves me."

"Good," he said. "Seat yourself there upon the mound, resting your head against the stone."

She obeyed; and taking thongs of hide which he had made ready, Hokosa bound her wrists and ankles, as these people bind the wrists and ankles of corpses. Then he knelt before her, staring into her face with his solemn eyes and muttering: "Obey and sleep."

Presently her limbs relaxed, and her head fell forward.

"Do you sleep?" he asked.

"I sleep. Whither shall I go? It is the true sleep—test me."

"Pass to the house of the white man, my rival. Are you with him?"

"I am with him."

"What does he?"

"He lies in slumber on his bed, and in his slumber he mutters the name of a woman, and tells her that he loves her, but that duty is more than love. Oh! call me back I cannot stay; a Presence guards him, and thrusts me thence."

"Return," said Hokosa starting. "Pass through the earth beneath you and tell me what you see."

"I see the body of the king; but were it not for his royal ornaments none would know him now."

"Return," said Hokosa, "and let the eyes of your spirit be open. Look around you and tell me what you see."

"I see the shadows of the dead," she answered; "they stand about you, gazing at you with angry eyes; but when they come near you, something drives them back, and I cannot understand what it is they say."

"Is the ghost of Umsuka among them?"

"It is among them."

"Bid him prophesy the future to me."

"I have bidden him, but he does not answer. If you would hear him speak, it must be through the lips of my body; and first my body must be emptied of my ghost, that his may find a place therein."

"Say, can his spirit be compelled?"

"It can be compelled, or that part of it which still hover near this spot, if you dare to speak the words you know. But first its house must be made ready. Then the words must be spoken, and all must be done before a man can count three hundred; for should the blood begin to clot about my heart, it will be still for ever."

"Hearken," said Hokosa. "When the medicine that I shall give does its work, and the spirit is loosened from your body, let it not go afar, no, whatever tempts or threatens it, and suffer not that the death-cord be severed, lest flesh and ghost be parted for ever."

"I hear, and I obey. Be swift, for I grow weary."

Then Hokosa took from his pouch two medicines: one a paste in a box, the other a fluid in a gourd. Taking of the paste he knelt upon the grave before the entranced woman and swiftly smeared it upon the mucous membrane of the mouth and throat. Also he thrust pellets of it into the ears, the nostrils, and the corners of the eyes.

The effect was almost instantaneous. A change came over the girl's lovely face, the last awful change of death. Her cheeks fell in, her chin dropped, her eyes opened, and her flesh quivered convulsively. The wizard saw it all by the bright moonlight. Then he took up his part in this unholy drama.

All that he did cannot be described, because it is indescribable. The Witch of Endor repeated no formula, but she raised the dead; and so did Hokosa the wizard. But he buried his face in the grey dust of the grave, he blew with his lips into the dust, he clutched at the dust with his hands, and when he raised his face again, lo! it was grey like the dust. Now began the marvel; for, though the woman before him remained a corpse, from the lips of that corpse a voice issued, and its sound was horrible, for the accent and tone of it were masculine, and the instrument through which it spoke—Noma's throat—was feminine. Yet it could be recognised as the voice of Umsuka the dead king.

"Why have you summoned me from my rest, Hokosa?" muttered the voice from the lips of the huddled corpse.

"Because I would learn the future, Spirit of the king," answered the wizard boldly, but saluting as he spoke. "You are dead, and to your sight all the Gates are opened. By the power that I have, I command you to show me what you see therein concerning myself, and to point out to me the path that I should follow to attain my ends and the ends of her in whose breast you dwell."

At once the answer came, always in the same horrible voice:—

"Hearken to your fate for this world, Hokosa the wizard. You shall triumph over your rival, the white man, the messenger; and by your hand he shall perish, passing to his appointed place where you must meet again. By that to which you cling you shall be betrayed, ah! you shall lose that which you love and follow after that which you do not desire. In the grave of error you shall find truth, from the deeps of sin you shall pluck righteousness. When these words fall upon your ears again, then, Wizard, take them for a sign and let your heart be turned. That which you deem accursed shall lift you up on high. High shall you be set above the nation and its king, and from age to age the voice of the people shall praise you. Yet in the end comes judgment; and there shall the sin and the atonement strive together, and in that hour, Wizard, you shall—"

Thus the voice spoke, strongly at first, but growing ever more feeble as the sparks of life departed from the body of the woman, till at length it ceased altogether.

"What shall chance to me in that hour?" Hokosa asked eagerly, placing his ears against Noma's lips.

No answer came; and the wizard knew that if he would drag his wife back from the door of death he must delay no longer. Dashing the sweat from his eyes with one hand, with the other he seized the gourd of fluid that he had placed ready, and thrusting back her head, he poured of its contents down her throat and waited a while. She did not move. In an extremity of terror he snatched a knife, and with a single cut severed a vein in her arm, then taking some of the fluid that remained in the gourd in his hand, he rubbed it roughly upon her brow and throat and heart. Now Noma's fingers stirred, and now, with horrible contortions and every symptom of agony, life returned to her. The blood flowed from her wounded arm, slowly at first, then more fast, and lifting her head she spoke.

"Take me hence," she cried, "or I shall go mad; for I have seen and heard things too terrible to be spoken!"

"What have you seen and heard?" he asked, while he cut the thongs which bound her wrists and feet.

"I do not know," Noma answered weeping; "the vision of them passes from me; but all the distances of death were open to my sight; yes, I travelled through the distances of death. In them I met him who was the king, and he lay cold within me, speaking to my heart; and as he passed from me he looked upon the child which I shall bear and cursed it, and surely accursed it shall be. Take me hence, O you most evil man, for of your magic I have had enough, and from this day forth I am haunted!"

"Have no fear," answered Hokosa; "you have made the journey whence but few return; and yet, as I promised you, you have returned to wear the greatness you desire and that I sent you forth to win; for henceforth we shall be great. Look, the dawn is breaking—the dawn of life and the dawn of power—and the mists of death and of disgrace roll back before us. Now the path is clear, the dead have shown it to me, and of wizardry I shall need no more."

"Ay!" answered Noma, "but night follows dawn as the dawn follows night; and through the darkness and the daylight, I tell you, Wizard, henceforth I am haunted! Also, be not so sure, for though I know not what the dead have spoken to you, yet it lingers on my mind that their words have many meanings. Nay, speak to me no more, but let us fly from this dread home of ghosts, this habitation of the spirit-folk which we have violated."

So the wizard and his wife crept from that solemn place, and as they went they saw the dawn-beams lighting upon the white cross that was reared in the Plain of Fire.

CHAPTER XII

THE MESSAGE OF HOKOSA

The weeks passed by, and Hokosa sat in his kraal weaving a great plot. None suspected him any more, for though he did not belong to it, he was heard to speak well of the new faith, and to acknowledge that the god of fire which he had worshipped was a false god. He was humble also towards the king, but he craved to withdraw himself from all matters of the State, saying that now he had but one desire—to tend his herds and garden, and to grow old in peace with the new wife whom he had chosen and whom he loved. Owen, too, he greeted courteously when he met him, sending him gifts of corn and cattle for the service of his church. Moreover, when a messenger came from Hafela, making proposals to him, he drove him away and laid the matter before the council of the king. Yet that messenger, who was hunted from the kraal, took back a secret word for Hafela's ear.

"It is not always winter," was the word, "and it may chance that in the springtime you shall hear from me." And again, "Say to the Prince Hafela, that though my face towards him is like a storm, yet behind the clouds the sun shines ever."

At length there came a day when Noma, his wife, was brought to bed. Hokosa, her husband, tended her alone, and when the child was born he groaned aloud and would not suffer her to look upon its face. Yet, lifting herself, she saw.

"Did I not tell you it was accursed?" she wailed. "Take it away!" and she sank back in a swoon. So he took the child, and buried it deep in the cattle-yard by night.

After this it came about that Noma, who, though her mind owned the sway of his, had never loved him over much, hated her husband Hokosa. Yet he had this power over her that she could not leave him. But he loved her more and more, and she had this power over him that she could always draw him to her. Great as her beauty had ever been, after the birth of the child it grew greater day by day, but it was an evil beauty, the beauty of a witch; and this fate fell upon her, that she feared the dark and would never be alone after the sun had set.

When she was recovered from her illness, Noma sat one night in her hut, and Hokosa sat there also watching her. The evening was warm, but a bright fire burned in the hut, and she crouched upon a stool by the fire, glancing continually over her shoulder.

"Why do you bide by the fire, seeing that it is so hot, Noma?" he asked.

"Because I fear to be away from the light," she answered; adding, "Oh, accursed man! for your own ends you have caused me to be bewitched, ah! and that which was born of me also, and bewitched I am by those shadows that you bade me seek, which now will never leave me. Nor, is this all. You swore to me that if I would do your will I should become great, ay! and you took me from one who would have made me great and whom I should have pushed on to victory. But now it seems that for nothing I made that awful voyage into the deeps of death; and for nothing, yet living, am I become the sport of those that dwell there. How am I greater than I was—I who am but the second wife of a fallen witch-doctor, who sits in the sun, day by day, while age gathers on his head like frost upon a bush? Where are all your high schemes now? Where is the fruit of wisdom that I gathered for you? Answer, Wizard, whom I have learned to hate, but from whom I cannot escape!"

"Truly," said Hokosa in a bitter voice, "for all my sins against them the heavens have laid a heavy fate upon my head, that thus with flesh and spirit I should worship a woman who loathes me. One comfort only is left to me, that you dare not take my life lest another should be added to those shadows who companion you, and what I bid you, that you must still do. Ay, you fear the dark, Noma; yet did I command you to rise and go stand alone through the long night yonder in the burying-place of kings, why, you must obey. Come, I command you—go!"

"Nay, nay!" she wailed in an extremity of terror. Yet she rose and went towards the door sideways, for her hands were outstretched in supplication to him.

"Come back," he said, "and listen: If a hunter has nurtured up a fierce dog, wherewith alone he can gain his livelihood, he tries to tame that dog by love, does he not? And if it will not become gentle, then, the brute being necessary to him, he tames it by fear. I am the hunter and, Noma, you are the hound; and since this curse is on me that I cannot live without you, why I must master you as best I may. Yet, believe me, I would not cause you fear or pain, and it saddens me that you should be haunted by these sick fancies, for they are nothing more. I have seen such cases before to-day, and I have noted that they can be cured by mixing with fresh faces and travelling in new countries. Noma, I think it would be well that, after your late sickness, according to the custom of the women of our people, you should part from me a while, and go upon a journey of purification."

"Whither shall I go and who will go with me?" she asked sullenly.

"I will find you companions, women discreet and skilled. And as to where you shall go, I will tell you. You shall go upon an embassy to the Prince Hafela."

"Are you not afraid that I should stop there?" she asked again, with a flash of her eyes. "It is true that I never learned all the story, yet I thought that the prince was not so glad to hand me back to you as you would have had me to believe. The price you paid for me must have been good, Hokosa, and mayhap it had to do with the death of a king."

"I am not afraid," he answered, setting his teeth, "because I know that whatever your heart may desire, my will follows you, and while I live that is a cord you cannot break unless I choose to loose it, Noma. I command you to be faithful to me and to return to me, and these commands you must obey. Hearken: you taunted me just now, saying that I sat like a dotard in the sun and advanced you nothing. Well, I will advance you, for both our sakes, but mostly for your own, since you desire it, and it must be done through the Prince Hafela. I cannot leave this kraal, for day and night I am watched, and before I had gone an hour's journey I should be seized; also here I have work to do. But the Place of Purification is secret, and when you reach it you need not bide there, you can travel on into the mountains till you come to the town of the Prince Hafela. He will receive you gladly, and you shall whisper this message in his ear:—

"'These are the words of Hokosa, my husband, which he has set in my mouth to deliver to you, O Prince. Be guided by them and grow great; reject them and die a wanderer, a little man of no account. But first, this is the price that you shall swear by the sacred oath to pay to Hokosa, if his wisdom finds favour in your sight and through it you come to victory: That after you, the king, he, Hokosa, shall be the first man in our land, the general of the armies, the captain of the council, the head of the doctors, and that to him shall be given half the cattle of Nodwengo, who now is king. Also to him shall be given power to stamp out the new faith which overruns the land like a foreign weed, and to deal as he thinks fit with those who cling thereto.'

"Now, Noma, when he has sworn this oath in your ear, calling down ruin upon his own head, should he break one word of it, and not before, you shall continue the message thus: 'These are the other words that Hokosa set in my mouth: "Know, O Prince, that the king, your brother, grows very strong, for he is a great soldier, who learned his art in bygone wars; also the white man that is named Messenger has taught him many things as to the building of forts and walls and the drilling and discipline of men. So strong is he that you can scarcely hope to conquer him in open war—yet snakes may crawl where men cannot walk. Therefore, Prince, let your part be that of a snake. Do you send an embassy to the king, your brother and say to him:—

"'My brother, you have been preferred before me and set up to be king in my place, and because of this my heart is bitter, so bitter that I have gathered my strength to make war upon you. Yet, at the last, I have taken another council, bethinking me that, if we fight, in the end it may chance that neither of us will be left alive to rule, and that the people also will be brought to nothing. To the north there lies a good country and a wide, where but few men live, and thither I would go, setting the mountains and the river between us; for there, far beyond your borders, I also can be a king. Now, to reach this country, I must travel by the pass that is not far from your Great Place, and I pray you that you will not attack my impis or the women and children that I shall send, and a guard before them, to await me in the plain beyond the mountains, seeing that these can only journey slowly. Let us pass by in peace, my brother, for so shall our quarrel be ended; but if you do so much as lift a single spear against me, then I will give you battle, setting my fortune against your fortune and my god against your God!'

"Such are the words that the embassy shall deliver into the ears of the king, Nodwengo, and it shall come about that when he hears them, Nodwengo, whose heart is gentle and who seeks not war, shall answer softly, saying:—

"'Go in peace, my brother, and live in peace in that land which you would win.'

"Then shall you, Hafela, send on the most of your cattle and the women and the children through that pass in the mountains, bidding them to await you in the plain, and after a while you shall follow them with your impis. But these shall not travel in war array, for carriers must bear their fighting shields in bundles and their stabbing spears shall be rolled up in mats. Now, on the sixth day of your journey you shall camp at the mouth of the pass which the cattle and the women have already travelled, and his outposts and spies will bring it to the ears of the king that your force is sleeping there, purposing to climb the pass on the morrow.

"But on that night, so soon as the darkness falls, you must rise up with your captains and your regiments, leaving your fires burning and men about your fires, and shall travel very swiftly across the valley, so that an hour before the dawn you reach the second range of mountains, and pass it by the gorge which is the burying-place of kings. Here you shall light a fire, which those who watch will believe to be but the fire of a herdsman who is acold. But I, Hokosa, also shall be watching, and when I see that fire I will creep, with some whom I can trust, to the little northern gate of the outer wall, and we will spear those that guard it and open the gate, that your army may pass through. Then, before the regiments can stand to their arms or those within it are awakened, you must storm the inner walls and by the light of the burning huts, put the dwellers in the Great Place to the spear, and the rays of the rising sun shall crown you king.

"Follow this counsel of mine, O Prince Hafela, and all will go well with you. Neglect it and be lost. There is but one thing which you need fear—it is the magic of the Messenger, to whom it is given to read the secret thoughts of men. But of him take no account, for he is my charge, and before ever you set a foot within the Great Place he shall have taken his answer back to Him Who sent him."

Hokosa finished speaking.

"Have you heard?" he said to Noma.

"I have heard."

"Then speak the message."

She repeated it word for word, making no fault. "Have no fear," she added, "I shall forget nothing when I stand before the prince."

"You are a woman, but your counsel is good. What think you of the plan, Noma?"

"It is deep and well laid," she answered, "and surely it would succeed were it not for one thing. The white man, Messenger, will be too clever for you, for as you say, he is a reader of the thoughts of men."

"Can the dead read men's thoughts, or if they can, do they cry them on the market-place or into the ears of kings?" asked Hokosa. "Have I not told you that, before I see the signal-fire yonder, the Messenger shall sleep sound? I have a medicine, Noma, a slow medicine that none can trace."

"The Messenger may sleep sound, Hokosa, and yet perchance he may pass on his message to another and, with it, his magic. Who can say? Still, husband, strike on for power and greatness and revenge, letting the blow fall where it will."

CHAPTER XIII

THE BASKET OF FRUIT

Three days later it was announced that according to the custom of the women of the People of Fire, Noma having given birth to a still-born child, was about to start upon a journey to the Mount of Purification. Here she would abide awhile and make sacrifice to the spirits of her ancestors, that they might cease to be angry with her and in future protect her from such misfortunes. This not unusual domestic incident excited little comment, although it was remarked that the four matrons by whom she was to be accompanied, in accordance with the tribal etiquette, were all of them the wives of soldiers who had deserted to Hafela. Indeed, the king himself noticed as much when Hokosa made the customary formal application to him to sanction the expedition.

"So be it," he said, "though myself I have lost faith in such rites. Also, Hokosa, I think it likely that although your wife goes out with company, she will return alone."

"Why, King?" asked Hokosa.

"For this reason—that those who travel with her have husbands yonder at the town of the Prince Hafela, and the Mount of Purification is on the road thither. Having gone so far, they may go farther. Well, let them go, for I desire to have none among my people whose hearts turn otherwise, and it would not be wonderful if they should choose to seek their lords. But perchance, Hokosa, there are some in this town who may use them as messengers to the prince"—and he looked at him keenly.

"I think not, King," said Hokosa. "None but a fool would make use of women to carry secret words or tidings. Their tongues are too long and their memories too bad, or too uncertain."

"Yet I have heard, Hokosa, that you have made use of women in many a strange work. Say now, what were you doing upon a night a while ago with that fair witch-wife if yours yonder in the burying-place of kings, where it is not lawful that you should set your foot? Nay, deny it not. You were seen to enter the valley after midnight and to return thence at the dawn, and it was seen also that as she came homewards your wife walked as one who is drunken, and she, whom it is not easy to frighten, wore a face of fear. Man, I do not trust you, and were I wise I should hunt you hence, or keep you so close that you could scarcely move without my knowledge.

"Why should I trust you?" Nodwengo went on vehemently. "Can a wizard cease from wizardry, or a plotter from his plots? No, not until the waters run upward and the sun shines at night; not until repentance touches you and your heart is changed, which I should hold as much a marvel. You were my father's friend and he made you great; yet you could plan with my brother to poison him, your king. Nay, be silent; I know it, though I have said nothing of it because one that is dear to me has interceded for you. You were the priest of the false god, and with that god are fallen from your place, yet you have not renounced him. You sit still in your kraal and pretend to be asleep, but your slumber is that of the serpent which watches his time to strike. How do I know that you will not poison me as you would have poisoned my father, or stir up rebellion against me, or bring my brother's impis on my head?"

"If the King thinks any of these things of his servant," answered Hokosa in a humble voice, but with dignity, "his path is plain: let him put me to death and sleep in peace. Who am I that I should full the ears of a king with my defence against these charges, or dare to wrangle with him?"

"Long ago I should have put you to death, Hokosa," answered Nodwengo sternly, "had it not been that one has pleaded for you, declaring that in you there is good which will overcome the evil, and that you who now are an axe to cut down my throne, in time to come shall be a roof-tree for its support. Also, the law that I obey does not allow me to take the blood of men save upon full proof, and against you as yet I have no proof. Still, Hokosa, be warned in time and let your heart be turned before the grave claims your body and the Wicked One your soul."

"I thank you, King, for your gentle words and your tender care for my well-being both on earth and after I shall leave it. But I tell you, King, that I had rather die as your father would have killed me in the old days, or your brother would kill me now, did either of them hate or fear me, than live on in safety, owing my life to a new law and a new mercy that do not befit the great ones of the world. King, I am your servant," and giving him the royal salute, Hokosa rose and left his presence.

"At the least there goes a man," said Nodwengo, as he watched him depart.

"Of whom do you speak, King?" asked Owen, who at that moment entered the royal house.

"Of him whom you must have touched in the door-way, Messenger, Hokosa the wizard," answered the king, and he told him of what had passed between them. "I said," he added, "that he was a man, and so he is; yet I hold that I have done wrong to listen to your pleading and to spare him, for I am certain that he will bring bloodshed upon me and trouble on the Faith. Think now, Messenger, how full must be that man's heart of secret rage and hatred, he who was so great and is now so little! Will he not certainly strive to grow great again? Will he not strive to be avenged upon those who humbled him and the religion they have chosen?"

"It may be," answered Owen, "but if so, he will not conquer. I tell you, King, that like water hidden in a rock there is good in this man's heart, and that I shall yet find a rod wherewith to cause it to gush out and refresh the desert."

"It is more likely that he will find a spear wherewith to cause your blood to gush out and refresh the jackals," answered the king grimly; "but be it as you will. And now, what of your business?"

"This, King: John, my servant, has returned from the coast countries, and he brings me a letter saying that before long three white teachers will follow him to take up the work which I have begun. I pray that when they come, for my sake and for the sake of the truth that I have taught you, you will treat them kindly and protect them, remembering that at first they can know little of your language or your customs."

"I will indeed," said the king, with much concern. "But tell me, Messenger, why do you speak of yourself as of one who soon will be but a memory? Do you purpose to leave us?"

"No, King, but I believe that ere long I shall be recalled. I have given my message, my task is well-nigh ended and I must be turning home. Save for your sakes I do not sorrow at this, for to speak truth I grow very weary," and he smiled sadly.

Hokosa went home alarmed and full of bitterness, for he had never guessed that the "servant of the Messenger," as he called Nodwengo the King, knew so much about him and his plans. His fall was hard to him, but to be thus measured up, weighed, and contemptuously forgiven was almost more than he could bear. It was the white prophet who had done this thing; he had told Nodwengo of his, Hokosa's, share in the plot to murder the late King Umsuka, though how he came to know of that matter was beyond guessing. He had watched him, or caused him to be watched, when he went forth to consult spirits in the place of the dead; he had warned Nodwengo against him. Worst of all, he had dared to treat him with contempt; had pleaded for his life and safety, so that he was spared as men spare a snake from which the charmer has drawn the fangs. When they met in the gate of the king's house yonder this white thief, who had stolen his place and power, had even smiled upon him and greeted him kindly, and doubtless while he smiled, by aid of the magic he possessed, had read him through and gone on to tell the story to the king. Well, of this there should be an end; he would kill the Messenger, or himself be killed.

When Hokosa reached his kraal he found Noma sitting beneath a fruit tree that grew in it, idly employed in stringing beads, for the work of the household she left to his other wife, Zinti, an old and homely woman who thought more of the brewing of the beer and the boiling of the porridge than of religions or politics or of the will of kings. Of late Noma had haunted the shadow of this tree, for beneath it lay that child which had been born to her.

"Does it please the king to grant leave for my journey?" she asked, looking up.

"Yes, it pleases him."

"I am thankful," she answered, "for I think that if I bide here much longer, with ghosts and memories for company, I shall go mad," and she glanced at a spot near by, where the earth showed signs of recent disturbance.

"He gives leave," Hokosa went on, taking no notice of her speech, "but he suspects us. Listen—" and he told her of the talk that had passed between himself and the king.

"The white man has read you as he reads in his written books," she answered, with a little laugh. "Well, I said that he would be too clever for you, did I not? It does not matter to me, for to-morrow I go upon my journey, and you can settle it as you will."

"Ay!" answered Hokosa, grinding his teeth, "it is true that he has read me; but this I promise you, that all books shall soon be closed to him. Yet how is it to be done without suspicion or discovery? I know many poisons, but all of them must be administered, and let him work never so cunningly, he who gives a poison can be traced."

"Then cause some other to give it and let him bear the blame," suggested Noma languidly.

Hokosa made no answer, but walking to the gate of the kraal, which was open, he leaned against it lost in thought. As he stood thus he saw a woman advancing towards him, who carried on her head a small basket of fruit, and knew her for one of those whose business it was to wait upon the Messenger in his huts, or rather in his house, for by now he had built himself a small house, and near it a chapel. This woman saw Hokosa also and looked at him sideways, as though she would like to stop and speak to him, but feared to do so.

"Good morrow to you, friend," he said. "How goes it with your husband and your house?"

Now Hokosa knew well that this woman's husband had taken a dislike to her and driven her from his home, filling her place with one younger and more attractive. At the question the woman's lips began to tremble, and her eyes swam with tears.

"Ah! great doctor," she said, "why do you ask me of my husband? Have you not heard that he has driven me away and that another takes my place?"

"Do I hear all the gossip of this town?" asked Hokosa, with a smile. "But come in and tell me the story; perchance I may be able to help you, for I have charms to compel the fancy of such faithless ones."

The woman looked round, and seeing that there was no one in sight, she slipped swiftly through the gate of the kraal, which he closed behind her.

"Noma," said Hokosa, "here is one who tells me that her husband has deserted her, and who comes to seek my counsel. Bring her milk to drink."

"There are some wives who would not find that so great an evil," replied Noma mockingly, as she rose to do his bidding.

Hokosa winced at the sarcasm, and turning to his visitor, said:—

"Now tell me your tale; but say first, why are you so frightened?"

"I am frightened, master," she answered, "lest any should have seen me enter here, for I have become a Christian, and the Christians are forbidden to consult the witch-doctors, as we were wont to do. For my case, it is—"

"No need to set it out," broke in Hokosa, waving his hand. "I see it written on your face; your husband has put you away and loves another woman, your own half-sister whom you brought up from a child."

"Ah! master, you have heard aright."

"I have not heard, I look upon you and I see. Fool, am I not a wizard? Tell me—" and taking dust into his hand, he blew the grains this way and that, regarding them curiously. "Yes, it is so. Last night you crept to your husband's hut—do you remember, a dog growled at you as you passed the gate?—and there in front of the hut he sat with his new wife. She saw you coming, but pretending not to see, she threw her arms about his neck, kissing and fondling him before your eyes, till you could bear it no longer, and revealed yourself, upbraiding them. Then your rival taunted you and stirred up the man with bitter words, till at length he took a stick and beat you from the door, and there is a mark of it upon your shoulder."

"It is true, it is too true!" she groaned.

"Yes, it is true. And now, what do you wish from me?"

"Master, I wish a medicine to make my husband hate my rival and to draw his heart back to me."

"That must be a strong medicine," said Hokosa, "which will turn a man from one who is young and beautiful to one who is past her youth and ugly."

"I am as I am," answered the poor woman, with a touch of natural dignity, "but at least I have loved him and worked for him for fifteen long years."

"And that is why he would now be rid of you, for who cumbers his kraal with old cattle?"

"And yet at times they are the best, Master. Wrinkles and smooth skin seem strange upon one pillow," she added, glancing at Noma, who came from the hut carrying a bowl of milk in her hand.

"If you seek counsel," said Hokosa quickly, "why do you not go to the white man, that Messenger in whom you believe, and ask him for a potion to turn your husband's heart?"

"Master, I have been to him, and he is very good to me, for when I was driven out he gave me work to do and food. But he told me that he had no medicine for such cases, and that the Great Man in the sky alone could soften the breast of my husband and cause my sister to cease from her wickedness. Last night I went to see whether He would do it, and you know what befell me there."

"That befell you which befalls all fools who put their trust in words alone. What will you pay me, woman, if I give you the medicine which you seek?"

"Alas, master, I am poor. I have nothing to offer you, for when I would not stay in my husband's kraal to be a servant to his new wife, he took the cow and the five goats that belonged to me, as, I being childless, according to our ancient law he had the right to do."

"You are bold who come to ask a doctor to minister to you, bearing no fee in your hand," said Hokosa. "Yet, because I have pity on you, I will be content with very little. Give me that basket of fruit, for my wife has been sick and loves its taste."

"I cannot do that, Master," answered the woman, "for it is sent by my hand as a present to the Messenger, and he knows this and will eat of it after he has made prayer to-day. Did I not give it to him, it would be discovered that I had left it here with you."

"Then begone without your medicine," said Hokosa, "for I need such fruit."

The woman rose and said, looking at him wistfully:—

"Master, if you will be satisfied with other fruits of this same sort, I know where I can get them for you."

"When will you get them?"

"Now, within an hour. And till I return I will leave these in pledge with you; but these and no other I must give to the Messenger, for he has already seen them and might discover the difference; also I have promised so to do."

"As you will," said Hokosa. "If you are with the fruit within an hour, the medicine will be ready for you, a medicine that shall not fail."

CHAPTER XIV

THE EATING OF THE FRUIT

The woman slipped away secretly. When she had gone Hokosa bade his wife bring the basket of fruit into the hut.

"It is best that the butcher should kill the ox himself," she answered meaningly.

He carried in the basket and set it on the floor.

"Why do you speak thus, Noma?" he asked.

"Because I will have no hand in the matter, Hokosa. I have been the tool of a wizard, and won little joy therefrom. The tool of a murderer I will not be!"

"If I kill, it is for the sake of both of us," he said passionately.

"It may be so, Hokosa, or for the sake of the people, or for the sake of Heaven above—I do not know and do not care; but I say, do your own killing, for I am sure that even less luck will hang to it than hangs to your witchcraft."

"Of all women you are the most perverse!" he said, stamping his foot upon the ground.

"Thus you may say again before everything is done, husband; but if it be so, why do you love me and tie me to you with your wizardry? Cut the knot, and let me go my way while you go yours."

"Woman, I cannot; but still I bid you beware, for, strive as you will, my path must be your path. Moreover, till I free you, you cannot lift voice or hand against me."

Then, while she watched him curiously, Hokosa fetched his medicines and took from them some powder fine as dust and two tiny crowquills. Placing a fruit before him, he inserted one of these quills into its substance, and filling the second with the powder, he shook its contents into it and withdrew the tube. This process he repeated four times on each of the fruits, replacing them one by one in the basket. So deftly did he work upon them, that however closely they were scanned none could guess that they had been tampered with.

"Will it kill at once?" asked Noma.

"No, indeed; but he who eats these fruits will be seized on the third day with dysentery and fever, and these will cling to him till within seven weeks—or if he is very strong, three months—he dies. This is the best of poisons, for it works through nature and can be traced by none."

"Except, perchance, by that Spirit Whom the white man worships, and Who also works through nature, as you learned, Hokosa, when He rolled the lightning back upon your head, shattering your god and beating down your company."

Then of a sudden terror seized the wizard, and springing to his feet, he cursed his wife till she trembled before him.

"Vile woman, and double-faced!" he said, "why do you push me forward with one hand and with the other drag me back? Why do you whisper evil counsel into one ear and into the other prophesy of misfortunes to come? Had it not been for you, I should have let this business lie; I should have taken my fate and been content. But day by day you have taunted me with my fall and grieved over the greatness that you have lost, till at length you have driven me to this. Why cannot you be all good or all wicked, or at the least, through righteousness and sin, faithful to my interest and your own?"

"Because I hate you, Hokosa, and yet can strike you only through my tongue and your mad love for me. I am fast in your power, but thus at least I can make you feel something of my own pain. Hark! I hear that woman at the gate. Will you give her back the basket, or will you not? Whatever you may choose to do, do not say in after days that I urged you to the deed."

"Truly you are great-hearted!" he answered, with cold contempt; "one for whom I did well to enter into treachery and sin! So be it: having gone so far upon it, come what may, I will not turn back from this journey. Let in that fool!"

Presently the woman stood before them, bearing with her another basket of fruit.

"These are what you seek, Master," she said, "though I was forced to win them by theft. Now give me my own and the medicine and let me go."

He gave her the basket, and with it, wrapped in a piece of kidskin, some of the same powder with which he had doctored the fruits.

"What shall I do with this?" she asked.

"You must find means to sprinkle it upon your sister's food, and thereafter your husband shall come to hate even the sight of her."

"But will he come to love me again?"

Hokosa shrugged his shoulders.

"I know not," he answered; "that is for you to see to. Yet this is sure, that if a tree grows up before the house of a man, shutting it off from the sunlight, when that tree is cut down the sun shines upon his house again."

"It is nothing to the sun on what he shines," said the woman.

"If the saying does not please you, then forget it. I promise you this and no more, that very soon the man shall cease to turn to your rival."

"The medicine will not harm her?" asked the woman doubtfully. "She has worked me bitter wrong indeed, yet she is my sister, whom I nursed when she was little, and I do not wish to do her hurt. If only he will welcome me back and treat me kindly, I am willing even that she should dwell on beneath my husband's roof, bearing his children, for will they not be of my own blood?"

"Woman," answered Hokosa impatiently, "you weary me with your talk. Did I say that the charm would hurt her? I said that it would cause your husband to hate the sight of her. Now begone, taking or leaving it, and let me rest. If your mind is troubled, throw aside that medicine, and go soothe it with such sights as you saw last night."

On hearing this the woman sprang up, hid away the poison in her hair, and taking her basket of fruit, passed from the kraal as secretly as she had entered it.

"Why did you give her death-medicine?" asked Noma of Hokosa, as he stood staring after her. "Have you a hate to satisfy against the husband or the girl who is her rival?"

"None," he answered, "for they have never crossed my path. Oh, foolish woman! cannot you read my plan?"

"Not altogether, Husband."

"Listen then: this woman will give to her sister a medicine of which in the end she must die. She may be discovered or she may not, but it is certain that she will be suspected, seeing that the bitterness of the quarrel between them is known. Also she will give to the Messenger certain fruits, after eating of which he will be taken sick and in due time die, of just such a disease as that which carries off the woman's rival. Now, if any think that he is poisoned, which I trust none will, whom will they suppose to have poisoned him, though indeed they can never prove the crime?"

"The plan is clever," said Noma with admiration, "but in it I see a flaw. The woman will say that she had the drug from you, or, at the least, will babble of her visit to you."

"Not so," answered Hokosa, "for on this matter the greatest talker in the world would keep silence. Firstly, she, being a Christian, dare not own that she has visited a witch-doctor. Secondly, the fruit she brought in payment was stolen, therefore she will say nothing of it. Thirdly, to admit that she had medicine from me would be to admit her guilt, and that she will scarcely do even under torture, which by the new law it is not lawful to apply. Moreover, none saw her come here, and I should deny her visit."

"The plan is very clever," said Noma again.

"It is very clever," he repeated complacently; "never have I made a better one. Now throw those fruits to the she goats that are in the kraal, and burn the basket, while I go and talk to some in the Great Place, telling them that I have returned from counting my cattle on the mountain, whither I went after I had bowed the knee in the house of the king."

Two hours later, Hokosa, having made a wide detour and talked to sundry of his acquaintances about the condition of his cattle, might have been seen walking slowly along the north side of the Great Place towards his own kraal. His path lay past the chapel and the little house that Owen had built to dwell in. This house was furnished with a broad verandah, and upon it sat the Messenger himself, eating his evening meal. Hokosa saw him, and a great desire entered his heart to learn whether or no he had partaken of the poisoned fruit. Also it occurred to him that it would be wise if, before the end came, he could contrive to divert all possible suspicion from himself, by giving the impression that he was now upon friendly terms with the great white teacher and not disinclined even to become a convert to his doctrine.

For a moment he hesitated, seeking an excuse. One soon suggested itself to his ready mind. That very morning the king had told him not obscurely that Owen had pleaded for his safety and saved him from being put upon his trial on charges of witchcraft and murder. He would go to him, now at once, playing the part of a grateful penitent, and the White Man's magic must be keen indeed if it availed to pierce the armour of his practised craft.

So Hokosa went up and squatted himself down native fashion among a little group of converts who were waiting to see their teacher upon one business or another. He was not more than ten paces from the verandah, and sitting thus he saw a sight that interested him strangely. Having eaten a little of a dish of roasted meat, Owen put out his hand and took a fruit from a basket that the wizard knew well. At this moment he looked up and recognised Hokosa.

"Do you desire speech with me, Hokosa?" he asked in his gentle voice. "If so, be pleased to come hither."

"Nay, Messenger," answered Hokosa, "I desire speech with you indeed, but it is ill to stand between a hungry man and his food."

"I care little for my food," answered Owen; "at the least it can wait," and he put down the fruit.

Then suddenly a feeling to which the wizard had been for many years a stranger took possession of him—a feeling of compunction. That man was about to partake of what would cause his death—of what he, Hokosa, had prepared in order that it should cause his death. He was good, he was kindly, none could allege a wrong deed against him; and, foolishness though it might be, so was the doctrine that he taught. Why should he kill him? It was true that never till that moment had he hesitated, by fair means or foul, to remove an enemy or rival from his path. He had been brought up in this teaching; it was part of the education of wizards to be merciless, for they reigned by terror and evil craft. Their magic lay chiefly in clairvoyance and powers of observation developed to a pitch that was almost superhuman, and the best of their weapons was poison in infinite variety, whereof the guild alone understood the properties and preparation. Therefore there was nothing strange, nothing unusual in this deed of devilish and cunning murder that the sight of its doing should stir him thus, and yet it did stir him. He was minded to stop the plot, to let things take their course.

Some sense of the futility of all such strivings came home to him, and as in a glass, for Hokosa was a man of imagination, he foresaw their end. A little success, a little failure, it scarcely mattered which, and then—that end. Within twenty years, or ten, or mayhap even one, what would this present victory or defeat mean to him? Nothing so far as he was concerned; that is, nothing so far as his life of to-day was concerned. Yet, if he had another life, it might mean everything. There was another life; he knew it, who had dragged back from its borders the spirits of the dead, though what might be the state and occupations of those dead he did not know. Yet he believed—why he could not tell—that they were affected vitally by their acts and behaviour here; and his intelligence warned him that good must always flow from good, and evil from evil. To kill this man was evil, and of it only evil could come.

What did he care whether Hafela ruled the nation or Nodwengo, and whether it worshipped the God of the Christians or the god of Fire—who, by the way, had proved himself so singularly inefficient in the hour of trial. Now that he thought of it, he much preferred Nodwengo to Hafela, for the one was a just man and the other a tyrant; and he himself was more comfortable as a wealthy private person than he had been as a head medicine-man and a chief of wizards. He would let things stand; he would prevent the Messenger from eating of that fruit. A word could do it; he had but to suggest that it was unripe or not wholesome at this season of the year, and it would be cast aside.

All these reflections, or their substance, passed through Hokosa's mind in a few instants of time, and already he was rising to go to the verandah and translate their moral into acts, when another thought occurred to him—How should he face Noma with this tale? He could give up his own ambitions, but could he bear her mockery, as day by day she taunted him with his faint-heartedness and reproached him with his failure to regain greatness and to make her great? He forgot that he might conceal the truth from her; or rather, he did not contemplate such concealment, of which their relations were too peculiar and too intimate to permit. She hated him, and he worshipped her with a half-inhuman passion—a passion so unnatural, indeed, that it suggested the horrid and insatiable longings of the damned—and yet their souls were naked to each other. It was their fate that they could hide nothing each from each—they were cursed with the awful necessity of candour.

It would be impossible that he should keep from Noma anything that he did or did not do; it would be still more impossible that she should conceal from him even such imaginings and things as it is common for women to hold secret. Her very bitterness, which it had been policy for her to cloak or soften, would gush from her lips at the sight of him; nor, in the depth of his rage and torment, could he, on the other hand, control the ill-timed utterance of his continual and overmastering passion. It came to this, then: he must go forward, and against his better judgment, because he was afraid to go back, for the whip of a woman's tongue drove him on remorselessly. It was better that the Messenger should die, and the land run red with blood, than that he should be forced to endure this scourge.

So with a sigh Hokosa sank back to the ground and watched while Owen ate three of the poisoned fruits. After a pause, he took a fourth and bit into it, but not seeming to find it to his taste, he threw it to a child that was waiting by the verandah for any scraps which might be left over from his meal. The child caught it, and devoured it eagerly.

Then, smiling at the little boy's delight, the Messenger called to Hokosa to come up and speak with him.

CHAPTER XV

NOMA COMES TO HAFELA

Hokosa advanced to the verandah and bowed to the white man with grave dignity.

"Be seated," said Owen. "Will you not eat? though I have nothing to offer you but these," and he pushed the basket of fruits towards him, adding, "The best of them, I fear, are already gone."

"I thank you, no, Messenger; such fruits are not always wholesome at this season of the year. I have known them to breed dysentery."

"Indeed," said Owen. "If so, I trust that I may escape. I have suffered from that sickness, and I think that another bout of it would kill me. In future I will avoid them. But what do you seek with me, Hokosa? Enter and tell me," and he led the way into a little sitting-room.

"Messenger," said the wizard, with deep humility, "I am a proud man; I have been a great man, and it is no light thing to me to humble myself before the face of my conqueror. Yet I am come to this. To-day when I was in audience with the king, craving a small boon of his graciousness, he spoke to me sharp and bitter words. He told me that he had been minded to put me on trial for my life because of various misdoings which are alleged against me in the past, but that you had pleaded for me and that for this cause he spared me. I come to thank you for your gentleness, Messenger, for I think that had I been in your place I should have whispered otherwise in the ear of the king."

"Say no more of it, friend," said Owen kindly, "We are all of us sinners, and it is my place to push back your ancient sins, not to drag them into the light of day and clamour for their punishment. It is true I know that you plotted with the Prince Hafela to poison Umsuka the King, for it was revealed to me. It chanced, however, that I was able to recover Umsuka from his sickness, and Hafela is fled, so why should I bring up the deed against you? It is true that you still practise witchcraft, and that you hate and strive against the holy Faith which I preach; but you were brought up to wizardry and have been the priest of another creed, and these things plead for you.

"Also, Hokosa, I can see the good and evil struggling in your soul, and I pray and I believe that in the end the good will master the evil; that you who have been pre-eminent in sin will come to be pre-eminent in righteousness. Oh! be not stubborn, but listen with your ear, and let your heart be softened. The gate stands open, and I am the guide appointed to show you the way without reward or fee. Follow them ere it be too late, that in time to come when my voice is stilled you also may be able to direct the feet of wanderers into the paths of peace. It is the hour of prayer; come with me, I beg of you, and listen to some few words of the message of my lips, and let your spirit be nurtured with them, and the Sun of Truth arise upon its darkness."

Hokosa heard, and before this simple eloquence his wisdom sank confounded. More, his intelligence was stirred, and a desire came upon him to investigate and examine the canons of a creed that could produce such men as this. He made no answer, but waiting while Owen robed himself, he followed him to the chapel. It was full of new-made Christians who crowded even the doorways, but they gave place to him, wondering. Then the service began—a short and simple service. First Owen offered up some prayer for the welfare of the infant Church, for the conversion of the unbelieving, for the safety of the king and the happiness of the people. Then John, the Messenger's first disciple, read aloud from a manuscript a portion of the Scripture which his master had translated. It was St. Paul's exposition of the resurrection from the dead, and the grandeur of its thoughts and language were by no means lost upon Hokosa, who, savage and heathen though he might be, was also a man of intellect.

The reading over, Owen addressed the congregation, taking for his text, "Thy sin shall find thee out." Being now a master of the language, he preached very well and earnestly, and indeed the subject was not difficult to deal with in the presence of an audience many of whose pasts had been stepped in iniquities of no common kind. As he talked of judgment to come for the unrepentant, some of his hearers groaned and even wept; and when, changing his note, he dwelt upon the blessed future state of those who earned forgiveness, their faces were lighted up with joy.

But perhaps among all those gathered before him there were none more deeply interested than Hokosa and one other, that woman to whom he had sold the poison, and who, as it chanced, sat next to him. Hokosa, watching her face as he was skilled to do, saw the thrusts of the preacher go home, and grew sure that already in her jealous haste she had found opportunity to sprinkle the medicine upon her rival's food. She believed it to be but a charm indeed, yet knowing that in using such charms she had done wickedly, she trembled beneath the words of denunciation, and rising at length, crept from the chapel.

"Truly, her sin will find her out," thought Hokosa to himself, and then in a strange half-impersonal fashion he turned his thoughts to the consideration of his own case. Would his sin find him out? he wondered. Before he could answer that question, it was necessary first to determine whether or no he had committed a sin. The man before him—that gentle and yet impassioned man—bore in his vitals the seed of death which he, Hokosa, had planted there. Was it wrong to have done this? It depended by which standard the deed was judged. According to his own code, the code on which he had been educated and which hitherto he had followed with exactness, it was not wrong. That code taught the necessity of self-aggrandisement, or at least and at all costs the necessity of self-preservation. This white preacher stood in his path; he had humiliated him, Hokosa, and in the end, either of himself or through his influences, it was probable that he would destroy him. Therefore he must strike before in his own person he received a mortal blow, and having no other means at his command, he struck through treachery and poison.

That was his law which for many generations had been followed and respected by his class with the tacit assent of the nation. According to this law, then, he had done no wrong. But now the victim by the altar, who did not know that already he was bound upon the altar, preached a new and a very different doctrine under which, were it to be believed, he, Hokosa, was one of the worst of sinners. The matter, then, resolved itself to this: which of these two rules of life was the right rule? Which of them should a man follow to satisfy his conscience and to secure his abiding welfare? Apart from the motives that swayed him, as a mere matter of ethics, this problem interested Hokosa not a little, and he went homewards determined to solve it if he might. That could be done in one way only—by a close examination of both systems. The first he knew well; he had practised it for nearly forty years. Of the second he had but an inkling. Also, if he would learn more of it he must make haste, seeing that its exponent in some short while would cease to be in a position to set it out.

"I trust that you will come again," said Owen to Hokosa as they left the chapel.

"Yes, indeed, Messenger," answered the wizard; "I will come every day, and if you permit it, I will attend your private teachings also, for I accept nothing without examination, and I greatly desire to study this new doctrine of yours, root and flower and fruit."

On the morrow Noma started upon her journey. As the matrons who accompanied her gave out with a somewhat suspicious persistency, its ostensible object was to visit the Mount of Purification, and there by fastings and solitude to purge herself of the sin of having given birth to a stillborn child. For amongst savage peoples such an accident is apt to be looked upon as little short of a crime, or, at the least, as indicating that the woman concerned is the object of the indignation of spirits who need to be appeased. To this Mount, Noma went, and there performed the customary rites.

"Little wonder," she thought to herself, "that the spirits were angry with her, seeing that yonder in the burying-ground of kings she had dared to break in upon their rest."

From the Place of Purification she travelled on ten days' journey with her companions till they reached the mountain fastness where Hafela had established himself. The town and its surroundings were of extraordinary strength, and so well guarded that it was only after considerable difficulty and delay that the women were admitted. Hearing of her arrival and that she had words for him, Hafela sent for Noma at once, receiving her by night and alone in his principal hut. She came and stood before him, and he looked at her beauty with admiring eyes, for he could not forget the woman whom the cunning of Hokosa had forced him to put away.

"Whence come you, pretty one?" he asked, "and wherefore come you? Are you weary of your husband, that you fly back to me? If so, you are welcome indeed; for know, Noma, that I still love you."

"Ay, Prince, I am weary of my husband sure enough; but I do not fly to you, for he holds me fast to him with bonds that you cannot understand, and fast to him while he lives I must remain."

"What hinders, Noma, that having got you here I should keep you here? The cunning and magic of Hokosa may be great, but they will need to be still greater to win you from my arms."

"This hinders, Prince, that you are playing for a higher stake than that of a woman's love, and if you deal thus by me and my husband, then of a surety you will lose the game."

"What stake, Noma?"

"The stake of the crown of the People of Fire."

"And why should I lose if I take you as a wife?"

"Because Hokosa, seeing that I do not return and learning from his spies why I do not return, will warn the king, and by many means bring all your plans to nothing. Listen now to the words of Hokosa that he has set between my lips to deliver to you"—and she repeated to him all the message without fault or fail.

"Say it again," he said, and she obeyed.

Then he answered:—

"Truly the skill of Hokosa is great, and well he knows how to set a snare; but I think that if by his counsel I should springe the bird, he will be too clever a man to keep upon the threshold of my throne. He who sets one snare may set twain, and he who sits by the threshold may desire to enter the house of kings wherein there is no space for two to dwell."

"Is this the answer that I am to take back to Hokosa?" asked Noma. "It will scarcely bind him to your cause, Prince, and I wonder that you dare to speak it to me who am his wife."

"I dare to speak it to you, Noma, because, although you be his wife, all wives do not love their lords; and I think that, perchance in days to come, you would choose rather to hold the hand of a young king than that of a witch-doctor sinking into eld. Thus shall you answer Hokosa: You shall say to him that I have heard his words and that I find them very good, and will walk along the path which he has made. Here before you I swear by the oath that may not be broken—the sacred oath, calling down ruin upon my head should I break one word of it—that if by his aid I succeed in this great venture, I will pay him the price he asks. After myself, the king, he shall be the greatest man among the people; he shall be general of the armies; he shall be captain of the council and head of the doctors, and to him shall be given half the cattle of Nodwengo. Also, into his hand I will deliver all those who cling to this faith of the Christians, and, if it pleases him, he shall offer them as a sacrifice to his god. This I swear, and you, Noma, are witness to the oath. Yet it may chance that after he, Hokosa, has gathered up all this pomp and greatness, he himself shall be gathered up by Death, that harvest-man whom soon or late will garner every ear;" and he looked at her meaningly.

"It may be so, Prince," she answered.

"It may be so," he repeated, "and when—"

"When it is so, then, Prince, we will talk together, but not till then. Nay, touch me not, for were he to command me, Hokosa has this power over me that I must show him all that you have done, keeping nothing back. Let me go now to the place that is made ready for me, and afterwards you shall tell me again and more fully the words that I must say to Hokosa my husband."

On the morrow Hafela held a secret council of his great men, and the next day an embassy departed to Nodwengo the king, taking to him that message which Hokosa, through Noma his wife, had put into the lips of the prince. Twenty days later the embassy returned saying that it pleased the king to grant the prayer of his brother Hafela, and bringing with it the tidings that the white man, Messenger, had fallen sick, and it was thought that he would die.

So in due course the women and children of the people of Hafela started upon their journey towards the new land where it was given out that they should live, and with them went Noma, purposing to leave them as they drew near the gates of the Great Place of the king. A while after, Hafela and his impis followed with carriers bearing their fighting shields in bundles, and having their stabbing spears rolled up in mats.

CHAPTER XVI

THE REPENTANCE OF HOKOSA

Hokosa kept his promise. On the morrow of his first attendance there he was again to be seen in the chapel, and after the service was over he waited on Owen at his house and listened to his private teaching. Day by day he appeared thus, till at length he became master of the whole doctrine of Christianity, and discovered that that which at first had struck him as childish and even monstrous, now presented itself to him in a new and very different light. The conversion of Hokosa came upon him through the gate of reason, not as is usual among savages—and some who are not savage—by that of the emotions. Given the position of a universe torn and groaning beneath the dual rule of Good and Evil, two powers of well-nigh equal potency, he found no great difficulty in accepting this tale of the self-sacrifice of the God of Good that He might wring the race He loved out of the conquering grasp of the god of Ill. There was a simple majesty about this scheme of redemption which appealed to one side of his nature. Indeed, Hokosa felt that under certain conditions and in a more limited fashion he would have been capable of attempting as much himself.

Once his reason was satisfied, the rest followed in a natural sequence. Within three weeks from the hour of his first attendance at the chapel Hokosa was at heart a Christian.

He was a Christian, although as yet he did not confess it; but he was also the most miserable man among the nation of the Sons of Fire. The iniquities of his past life had become abominable to him; but he had committed them in ignorance, and he understood that they were not beyond forgiveness. Yet high above them all towered one colossal crime which, as he believed, could never be pardoned to him in this world or the next. He was the treacherous murderer of the Messenger of God; he was in the very act of silencing the Voice that had proclaimed truth in the dark places of his soul and the dull ears of his countrymen.

The deed was done; no power on earth could save his victim. Within a week from the day of eating that fatal fruit Owen began to sicken, then the dysentery had seized him which slowly but surely was wasting out his life. Yet he, the murderer, was helpless, for with this form of the disease no medicine could cope. With agony in his heart, an agony that was shared by thousands of the people, Hokosa watched the decrease of the white man's strength, and reckoned the days that would elapse before the end. Having such sin as thus upon his soul, though Owen entreated him earnestly, he would not permit himself to be baptised. Twice he went near to consenting, but on each occasion an ominous and terrible incident drove him from the door of mercy.

Once, when the words "I will" were almost on his lips, a woman broke in upon their conference bearing a dying boy in her arms.

"Save him," she implored, "save him, Messenger, for he is my only son!"

Owen looked at him and shook his head.

"How came he like this?" he asked.

"I know not, Messenger, but he has been sick ever since he ate of a certain fruit which you gave to him;" and she recalled to his mind the incident of the throwing of a fruit to the child, which she had witnessed.

"I remember," said Owen. "It is strange, but I also have been sick from the day that I ate of those fruits; yes, and you, Hokosa, warned me against them."

Then he blessed the boy and prayed over him till he died; but when afterwards he looked round for Hokosa, it was to find that he had gone.

Some eight days later, having to a certain extent recovered from this shock, Hokosa went one morning to Owen's house and talked to him.

"Messenger," he said, "is it necessary to baptism that I should confess all my sins to you? If so, I can never be baptised, for there is wickedness upon my hands which I am unable to tell into the ear of living man."

Owen thought and answered:—

"It is necessary that you should repent all of your sins, and that you should confess them to heaven; it is not necessary that you should confess them to me, who am but a man like yourself."

"Then I will be baptised," said Hokosa with a sigh of relief.

At this moment, as it chanced, their interview was again interrupted, for runners came from the king requesting the immediate presence of the Messenger, if he were well enough to attend, upon a matter connected with the trial of a woman for murder. Thinking that he might be of service, Owen, leaning on the shoulder of Hokosa, for already he was too weak to walk far, crept to the litter which was waiting for him, and was borne to the place of judgment that was before the house of the king. Hokosa followed, more from curiosity than for any other reason, for he had heard of no murder being committed, and his old desire to be acquainted with everything that passed was still strong on him. The people made way for him, and he seated himself in the first line of spectators immediately opposite to the king and three other captains who were judges in the case. So soon as Owen had joined the judges, the prisoner was brought before them, and to his secret horror Hokosa recognised in her that woman to whom he had given the poison in exchange for the basket of fruit.

Now it seemed to Hokosa that his doom was on him, for she would certainly confess that she had the drug from him. He thought of flight only to reject the thought, for to fly would be to acknowledge himself an accessory. No, he would brazen it out, for after all his word was as good as hers. With the prisoner came an accuser, her husband, who seemed sick, and he it was who opened the case against her.

"This woman," he said, "was my wife. I divorced her for barrenness, as I have a right to do according to our ancient law, and I took another woman to wife, her half-sister. This woman was jealous; she plagued me continually, and insulted her sister, so that I was forced to drive her away. After that she came to my house, and though they said nothing of it at the time, she was seen by two servants of mine to sprinkle something in the bowl wherein our food was cooking. Subsequently my wife, this woman's half-sister, was taken ill with dysentery. I also was taken ill with dysentery, but I still live to tell this story before you, O King, and your judges, though I know not for how long I live. My wife died yesterday, and I buried her this morning. I accuse the woman of having murdered her, either by witchcraft or by means of a medicine which she sprinkled on the food, or by both. I have spoken."

"Have you anything to say?" asked the king of the prisoner. "Are you guilty of the crime whereof this man who was your husband charges you, or does he lie?"

Then the woman answered in a low and broken voice:—

"I am guilty, King. Listen to my story:" and she told it all as she told it to Hokosa. "I am guilty," she added, "and may the Great Man in the sky, of Whom the Messenger has taught us, forgive me. My sister's blood is upon my hands, and for aught I know the blood of my husband yonder will also be on my hands. I seek no mercy; indeed, it is better that I should die; but I would say this in self-defence, that I did not think to kill my sister. I believed that I was giving to her a potion which would cause her husband to hate her and no more."

Here she looked round and her eyes met those of Hokosa.

"Who told you that this was so?" asked one of the judges.

"A witch-doctor," she answered, "from whom I bought the medicine in the old days, long ago, when Umsuka was king."

Hokosa gasped. Why should this woman have spared him?

No further question was asked of her, and the judges consulted together. At length the king spoke.

"Woman," he said, "you are condemned to die. You will be taken to the Doom Tree, and there be hanged. Out of those who are assembled to try you, two, the Messenger and myself, have given their vote in favour of mercy, but the majority think otherwise. They say that a law has been passed against murder by means of witchcraft and secret medicine, and that should we let you go free, the people will make a mock of that law. So be it. Go in peace. To-morrow you must die, and may forgiveness await you elsewhere."

"I ask nothing else," said the woman. "It is best that I should die."

Then they led her away. As she passed Hokosa she turned and looked him full in the eyes, till he dropped his head abashed. Next morning she was executed, and he learned that her last words were: "Let it come to the ears of him who sold me the poison, telling me that it was but a harmless drug, that as I hope to be forgiven, so I forgive him, believing that my silence may win for him time for repentance, before he follows on the road I tread."

Now, when Hokosa heard these words he shut himself up in his house for three days, giving out that he was sick. Nor would he go near to Owen, being altogether without hope, and not believing that baptism or any other rite could avail to purge such crimes as his. Truly his sin had found him out, and the burden of it was intolerable. So intolerable did it become, that at length he determined to be done with it. He could live no more. He would die, and by his own hand, before he was called upon to witness the death of the man whom he had murdered. To this end he made his preparations. For Noma he left no message; for though his heart still hungered after her, he knew well that she hated him and would rejoice at his death.

When all was ready he sat down to think a while, and as he thought, a man entered his hut saying that the Messenger desired to see him. At first he was minded not to go, then it occurred to him that it would be well if he could die with a clean heart. Why should he not tell all to the white man, and before he could be delivered up to justice take that poison which he had prepared? It was impossible that he should be forgiven, yet he desired that his victim should learn how deep was his sorrow and repentance, before he proved it by preceding him to death. So he rose and went.

He found Owen in his house, lying in a rude chair and propped up by pillows of bark. Now he was wasted almost to a shadow, and in the pale pinched face his dark eyes, always large and spiritual, shone with unnatural lustre, while his delicate hands were so thin that when he held them up in blessing the light showed through them.

"Welcome, friend," he said. "Tell me, why have you deserted me of late? Have you been ill?"

"No, Messenger," answered Hokosa, "that is, not in my body. I have been sick at heart, and therefore I have not come."

"What, Hokosa, do your doubts still torment you? I thought that my prayers had been heard, and that power had been given me to set them at rest for ever. Man, let me hear the trouble, and swiftly, for cannot you who are a doctor see that I shall not be here for long to talk with you? My days are numbered, Hokosa, and my work is almost done."

"I know it," answered Hokosa. "And, Messenger, my days are also numbered."

"How is this?" asked Owen, "seeing that you are well and strong. Does an enemy put you in danger of your life?"

"Yes, Messenger, and I myself am that enemy; for to-day I, who am no longer fit to live, must die by my own hand. Nay, listen and you will say that I do well, for before I go I would tell you all. Messenger, you are doomed, are you not? Well, it was I who doomed you. That fruit which you ate a while ago was poisoned, and by my hand, for I am a master of such arts. From the beginning I hated you, as well I might, for had you not worsted me and torn power from my grasp, and placed the people and the king under the rule of another God? Therefore, when all else failed, I determined to murder you, and I did the deed by means of that woman who not long ago was hung for the killing of her sister, though in truth she was innocent." And he told him what had passed between himself and the woman, and told him also of the plot which he had hatched to kill Nodwengo and the Christians, and to set Hafela on the throne.

"She was innocent," he went on, "but I am guilty. How guilty you and I know alone. Do you remember that day when you ate the fruit, how after it I accompanied you to the church yonder and listened to your preaching? 'Your sin shall find you out,' you said, and of a surety mine has found me out. For, Messenger, it came about that in listening to you then and afterwards, I grew to love you and to believe the words you taught, and therefore am I of all men the most miserable, and therefore must I, who have been great and the councillor of kings, perish miserably by the death of a dog.

"Now curse me, and let me go."

CHAPTER XVII

THE LOOSING OF NOMA

When Owen heard that it was Hokosa who had poisoned him, he groaned and hid his face in his hands, and thus he remained till the evil tale was finished. Now he lifted his head and spoke, but not to Hokosa.

"O God," he said, "I thank Thee that at the cost of my poor life Thou hast been pleased to lead this sinner towards the Gate of Righteousness, and to save alive those whom Thou hast sent me to gather to Thy Fold."

Then he looked at Hokosa and said:—

"Unhappy man, is not your cup full enough of crime, and have you not sufficiently tempted the mercy of Heaven, that you would add to all your evil deeds that of self-murder?"

"It is better to die to-day by my own hand," answered Hokosa, "than to-morrow among the mockery of the people to fall a victim to your vengeance, Messenger."

"Vengeance! Did I speak to you of vengeance? Who am I that I should take vengeance upon one who has repented? Hokosa, freely do I forgive you all, even as in some few days I hope to be forgiven. Freely and fully from my heart do I forgive you, nor shall my lips tell one word of the sin that you have worked against me."

Now, when Hokosa heard those words, for a moment he stared stupefied; then he fell upon his knees before Owen, and bowing his head till it touched the teacher's feet, he burst into bitter weeping.

"Rise and hearken," said Owen gently. "Weep not because I have shown kindness to you, for that is my duty and no more, but for your sins in your own heart weep now and ever. Yet for your comfort I tell you that if you do this, of a surety they shall be forgiven to you. Hokosa, you have indeed lost that which you loved, and henceforth you must follow after that which you did not desire. In the very grave of error you have found truth, and from the depths of sin you shall pluck righteousness. Ay, that Cross which you deemed accursed shall lift you up on high, for by it you shall be saved."

Hokosa heard and shivered.

"Who set those words between your lips, Messenger?" he whispered.

"Who set them, Hokosa? Nay, I know not—or rather, I know well. He set them Who teaches us to speak all things that are good."

"It must be so, indeed," replied Hokosa. "Yet I have heard them before; I have heard them from the lips of the dead, and with them went this command: that when they fell upon my ears again I should 'take them for a sign, and let my heart be turned.'"

"Tell me that tale," said Owen.

So he told him, and this time it was the white man who trembled.

"Horrible has been your witchcraft, O Son of Darkness!" said Owen, when he had finished; "yet it would seem that it was permitted to you to find truth in the pit of sorcery. Obey, obey, and let your heart be turned. The dead told you that you should be set high above the nation and its king, and that saying I cannot read, though it may be fulfilled in some fashion of which to-day you do not think. At the least, the other saying is true, that in the end comes judgment, and that there shall the sin and the atonement strive together; therefore for judgment prepare yourself. And now depart, for I must talk with the king as to this matter of the onslaught of Hafela."

"Then, that will be the signal for my death, for what king can forgive one who has plotted such treachery against him?" said Hokosa.

"Fear not," answered Owen, "I will soften his heart. Go you into the church and pray, for there you shall be less tempted; but before you go, swear to me that you will work no evil on yourself."

"I swear it, Messenger, since now I desire to live, if only for awhile, seeing that death shuts every door."

Then he went to the church and waited there. An hour later he was summoned, and found the king seated with Owen.

"Man," said Nodwengo, "I am told by the Messenger here that you have knowledge of a plot which my brother the Prince Hafela has made to fall treacherously upon me and put me and my people to the spear. How you come to be acquainted with the plot, and what part you have played in it, I will not now inquire, for so much have I promised to the Messenger. Yet I warn you it will be well that you should tell me all you know, and that should you lie to me or attempt to deceive me, then you shall surely die."

"King, hear all the truth," answered Hokosa in a voice of desperate calm. "I have knowledge of the plot, for it was I who wove it; but whether or not Hafela will carry it out altogether I cannot say, for as yet no word has reached me from him. King, this was the plan that I made." And he told him everything.

"It is fortunate for you, Hokosa," said Nodwengo grimly when he had finished, "that I gave my word to the Messenger that no harm should come to you, seeing that you have repented and confessed. This is certain, that Hafela has listened to your evil counsels, for I gave my consent to his flight from this land with all his people, and already his women and children have crossed the mountain path in thousands. Well, this I swear, that their feet shall tread it no more, for where they are thither he shall go to join them, should he chance to live to do so. Hokosa, begone, and know that day and night you will be watched. Should you so much as dare to approach one of the gates of the Great Place, that moment you shall die."

"Have no fear, O King," said Hokosa humbly, "for I have emptied all my heart before you. The past is the past, and cannot be recalled. For the future, while it pleases you to spare me, I am the most loyal of your servants."

"Can a man empty a spring with a pitcher?" asked the king contemptuously. "By to-morrow this heart of yours may be full again with the blackest treachery, O master of sin and lies. Many months ago I spared you at the prayer of the Messenger; and now at his prayer I spare you again, yet in doing so I think that I am foolish."

"Nay, I will answer for him," broke in Owen. "Let him stay here with me, and set your guard without my gates."

"How do I know that he will not murder you, friend?" asked the king. "This man is a snake whom few can nurse with safety."

"He will not murder me," said Owen smiling, "because his heart is turned from evil to good; also, there is little need to murder a dying man."

"Nay, speak not so," said the king hastily; "and as for this man, be it as you will. Come, I must take counsel with my captains, for our danger is near and great."

So it came about that Hokosa stayed in the house of Owen.

On the morrow the Great Place was full of the bustle of preparation, and by dawn of the following day an impi of some seventeen thousand spears had started to ambush Hafela and his force in a certain wooded defile through which he must pass on his way to the mountain pass where his women and children were gathered. The army was not large, at least in the eyes of the People of Fire who, before the death of Umsuka and the break up of the nation, counted their warriors by tens of thousands. But after those events the most of the regiments had deserted to Hafela, leaving to Nodwengo not more than two-and-twenty thousand spears upon which he could rely. Of these he kept less than a third to defend the Great Place against possible attacks, and all the rest he sent to fall upon Hafela far away, hoping there to make an end of him once and for all. This counsel the king took against the better judgment of many of his captains, and as the issue proved, it was mistaken.

When Owen told Hokosa of it, that old general shrugged his shoulders.

"The king would have done better to keep his regiments at home," he said, "and fight it out with Hafela here, where he is well prepared. Yonder the country is very wide, and broken, and it may well chance that the impi will miss that of Hafela, and then how can the king defend this place with a handful, should the prince burst upon him at the head of forty thousand men? But who am I that I should give counsel for which none seek?"

"As God wills, so shall it befall," answered Owen wearily; "but oh! the thought of all this bloodshed breaks my heart. I trust that its beatings may be stilled before my eyes behold the evil hour."

On the evening of that day Hokosa was baptised. The ceremony took place, not in the church, for Owen was too weak to go there, but in the largest room of his house and before some few witnesses chosen from the congregation. Even as he was being signed with the sign of the cross, a strange and familiar attraction caused the convert to look up, and behold, before him, watching all with mocking eyes, stood Noma his wife. At length the rite was finished, and the little audience melted away, all save Noma, who stood silent and beautiful as a statue, the light of mockery still gleaming in her eyes. Then she spoke, saying:—

"I greet you, Husband. I have returned from doing your business afar, and if this foolishness is finished, and the white man can spare you, I would talk with you alone."

"I greet you, Wife," answered Hokosa. "Say out your say, for none are present save us three, and from the Messenger here I have no secrets."

"What, Husband, none? Do you ever talk to him of certain fruit that you ripened in a garden yonder?"

"From the Messenger I have no secrets," repeated Hokosa in a heavy voice.

"Then his heart must be full of them indeed, and it is little wonder that he seems sick," replied Noma, gibing. "Tell me, Hokosa, is it true that you have become a Christian, or would you but fool the white man and his following?"

"It is true."

At the words her graceful shape was shaken with a little gust of silent laughter.

"The wizard has turned saint," she said. "Well, then, what of the wizard's wife?"

"You were my wife before I became Christian; if the Messenger permits it, you can still abide with me."

"If the Messenger permits it! So you have come to this, Hokosa, that you must ask the leave of another man as to whether or no you should keep your own wife! There is no other thing that I could not have thought of you, but this I would never have believed had I not heard it from your lips. Say now, do you still love me, Hokosa?"

"You know well that I love you, now and always," he answered, in a voice that sounded like a groan; "as you know that for love of you I have done many sins from which otherwise I should have turned aside."

"Grieve not over them, Hokosa; after all, in such a count as yours they will make but little show. Well, if you love me, I hate you, though through your witchcraft your will yet has the mastery of mine. I demand of you now that you should loose that bond, for I do not desire to become a Christian; and surely, O most good and holy man, having one wife already, it will not please you henceforth to live in sin with a heathen woman."

Now Hokosa turned to Owen:—

"In the old days," he said, "I could have answered her; but now I am fallen; or raised up—at the least I am changed and cannot. O prophet of Heaven, tell me what I shall do."

"Sever the bond that you have upon her and let her go," answered Owen. "This love of yours is unnatural, unholy and born of witchcraft; have done with it, or if you cannot, at the least deny it, for such a woman, a woman who hates you, can work you no good. Moreover, since she is a second wife, you being a Christian, are bound to free her should she so desire."

"She can work me no good, Messenger, that I know; but I know also that while she struggles in the net of my will she can work me no evil. If I loose the net and the fish swims free, it may be otherwise."

"Loose it," answered Owen, "and leave the rest to Providence. Henceforth, Hokosa, do right, and take no thought for the morrow, for the morrow is with God, and what He decrees, that shall befall."

"I hear you," said Hokosa, "and I obey." For a while he rocked himself to and fro, staring at the ground, then he lifted his head and spoke:—

"Woman," he said, "the knot is untied and the spell is broken. Begone, for I release you and I divorce you. Flesh of my flesh have you been, and soul of my soul, for in the web of sorceries are we knit together. Yet be warned and presume not too far, for remember that which I have laid down I can take up, and that should I choose to command, you must still obey. Farewell, you are free."

Noma heard, and with a sigh of ecstasy she sprang into the air as a slave might do from whom the fetters have been struck off.

"Ay," she cried, "I am free! I feel it in my blood, I who have lain in bondage, and the voice of freedom speaks in my heart and the breath of freedom blows in my nostrils. I am free from you, O dark and accursed man; but herein lies my triumph and revenge—you are not free from me. In obedience to that white fool whom you have murdered, you have loosed me; but you I will not loose and could not if I would. Listen now, Hokosa: you love me, do you not?—next to this new creed of yours, I am most of all to you. Well, since you have divorced me, I will tell you, I go straight to another man. Now, look your last on me; for you love me, do you not?" and she slipped the mantle from her shoulders and except for her girdle stood before him naked, and smiled.

"Well," she went on, resuming her robe, "the last words of those we love are always dear to us; therefore, Hokosa, you who were my husband, I leave mine with you. You are a coward and a traitor, and your doom shall be that of a coward and a traitor. For my sake you betrayed Umsuka, your king and benefactor; for your own sake you betrayed Nodwengo, who spared you; and now, for the sake of your miserable soul, you have betrayed Hafela to Nodwengo. Nay, I know the tale, do not answer me, but the end of it—ah! that is yet to learn. Lie there, snake, and lick the hand that you have bitten, but I, the bird whom you have loosed, I fly afar—taking your heart with me!" and suddenly she turned and was gone.

Presently Hokosa spoke in a thick voice:—

"Messenger," he said, "this cross that you have given me to bear is heavy indeed."

"Yes, Hokosa," answered Owen, "for to it your sins are nailed."

CHAPTER XVIII

THE PASSING OF OWEN

Once she was outside of Owen's house, Noma did not tarry. First she returned to Hokosa's kraal, where she had already learnt from his head wife, Zinti, and others the news of his betrayal of the plot of Hafela, of his conversion to the faith of the Christians, and of the march of the impi to ambush the prince. Here she took a little spear, and rolling up in a skin blanket as much dried meat as she could carry, she slipped unnoticed from the kraal. Her object was to escape from the Great Place, but this she did not try to do by any of the gates, knowing them to be guarded. Some months ago, before she started on her embassy, she had noted a weak spot in the fence, where dogs had torn a hole through which they passed out to hunt at night. To this spot she made her way under cover of the darkness—for though she still greatly feared to be alone at night, her pressing need conquered her fears—and found that the hole was yet there, for a tall weed growing in its mouth had caused it to be overlooked by those whose duty it was to mend the fence. With her assegai she widened it a little, then drew her lithe shape through it, and lying hidden till the guard had passed, climbed the two stone walls beyond. Once she was free of the town, she set her course by the stars and started forward at a steady run.

"If my strength holds I shall yet be in time to warn him," she muttered to herself. "Ah! friend Hokosa, this new madness of yours has blunted your wits that once were sharp enough. You have set me free, and now you shall learn how I can use my freedom. Not for nothing have I been your pupil, Hokosa the fox."

Before the dawn broke Noma was thirty miles from the Great Place, and before the next dawn she was a hundred. At sunset on that second day she stood among mountains. To her right stretched a great defile, a rugged place of rocks and bush, wherein she knew that the regiments of the king were hid in ambush. Perchance she was too late, perchance the impi of Hafela had already passed to its doom in yonder gorge. Swiftly she ran forward on to the trail which led to the gorge, to find that it had been trodden by many feet and recently. Moving to and fro she searched the spoor with her eyes, then rose with a sigh of joy. It was old, and marked the passage of the great company of women and children and their thousands of cattle which, in execution of the plot, had travelled this path some days before. Either the impi had not yet arrived, or it had gone by some other road. Weary as she was, Noma followed the old spoor backwards. A mile or more away it crossed the crest of a hog-backed mountain, from whose summit she searched the plain beyond, and not in vain, for there far beneath her twinkled the watch-fires of the army of Hafela.

Three hours later a woman, footsore and utterly exhausted, staggered into the camp, and waving aside the spears that were lifted to stab her, demanded to be led to the prince. Presently she was there.

"Who is this woman?" asked the great warrior; for, haggard as she was with travel, exhaustion, and the terror of her haunted loneliness, he did not know her in the uncertain firelight.

"Hafela," she said, "I am Noma who was the wife of Hokosa, and for whole nights and days I have journeyed as no woman ever journeyed before, to tell you of the treachery of Hokosa and to save you from your doom."

"What treachery and what doom?" asked the prince.

"Before I answer you that question, Hafela, you must pay me the price of my news."

"Let me hear the price, Noma."

"It is this, Prince: First, the head of Hokosa, who has divorced me, when you have caught him."

"That I promise readily. What more?"

"Secondly, the place of your chief wife to-day; and a week hence, when I shall have made you king, the name and state of Queen of the People of Fire with all that hangs thereto."

"You are ambitious, woman, and know well how to drive a bargain. Well, if you can ask, I can give, for I have ever loved you, and your mind is great as your body is beautiful. If through your help I should become King of the People of Fire, you shall be their Queen, I swear it by the spirits of my fathers and by my own head. And now—your tidings."

"These are they, Hafela. Hokosa has turned Christian and betrayed the plot to Nodwengo; and the great gorge yonder but three hours march away is ambushed. To-morrow you and your people would have been cut off there had I not run so fast and far to warn you, after which the impis of Nodwengo were commanded to follow your women and cattle over the mountain pass and capture them."

"This is news indeed," said the prince. "Say now, how many regiments are hidden in the gorge?"

"Eight."

"Well, I have fourteen; so, being warned, there is little to fear. I will catch these rats in their own hole."

"I have a better plan," said Noma; "it is this: leave six regiments posted upon the brow of yonder hill and let them stay there. Then when the generals of Nodwengo see that they do not enter the gorge, they will believe that the ambush is discovered, and, after waiting one day or perhaps two, will move out to give battle, thinking that before them is all your strength. But command your regiments to run and not to fight, drawing the army of Nodwengo after them. Meanwhile, yes, this very night, you yourself with all the men that are left to you must march upon the Great Place, which, though it be strong, can be stormed, for it is defended by less than five thousand soldiers. There, having taken it, you shall slay Nodwengo, proclaiming yourself king, and afterwards, by the help of the impi that you leave here which will march onward to your succour, you can deal with yonder army."

"A great scheme truly," said Hafela in admiration; "but how do I know whether all this tale is true, or whether you do but set a snare for me?"

"Bid scouts go out and creep into yonder gully," answered Noma, "and you will see whether or no I have spoken falsely. For the rest, I am in your hands, and if I lie you can take my life in payment."

"If I march upon the Great Place, it must be at midnight when none see me go," said Hafela, "and what will you do then, Noma, who are too weary to travel again so soon?"

"I will be borne in a litter till my strength comes back to me," she answered. "And now give me to eat and let me rest while I may."

Five hours later, Hafela with the most of his army, a force of something over twenty thousand men, was journeying swiftly but by a circuitous route towards the Great Place of the king. On the crest of the hill facing the gorge, as Noma had suggested, he left six regiments with instructions to fly before Nodwengo's generals, and when they had led them far enough, to follow him as swiftly as they were able. These orders, or rather the first part of them, they carried out, for as it chanced after two days' flight, the king's soldiers got behind them by a night march, and falling on them at dawn, killed half of them and dispersed the rest. Then it was that Nodwengo's generals learned for the first time that they were following one wing of Hafela's army only, while the main body was striking at the heart of the kingdom, and turned their faces homewards in fear and haste.

On the morning after the flight of Noma, Owen passed into the last stage of his sickness, and it became evident, both to himself and to those who watched him, that at the most he could not live for more than a few days. For his part, he accepted his doom joyfully, spending the time which was left to him in writing letters that were to be forwarded to England whenever an opportunity should arise. Also he set down on paper a statement of the principal events of his strange mission, and other information for the guidance of his white successors, who by now should be drawing near to the land of the Amasuka. In the intervals of these last labours, from time to time he summoned the king and the wisest and trustiest of them whom he had baptised to his bedside, teaching them what they should do when he was gone, and exhorting them to cling to the Faith.

On the afternoon of the fourth day from that of the baptism of Hokosa he fell into a quiet sleep, from which he did not wake till sundown.

"Am I still here?" he asked wondering, of John and Hokosa who watched at his bedside. "From my dreams I thought that it was otherwise. John, send a messenger to the king and ask of him to assemble the people, all who care to come, in the open place before my house. I am about to die, and first I would speak with them."

John went weeping upon his errand, leaving Owen and Hokosa alone.

"Tell me know what shall I do?" said Hokosa in a voice of despair, "seeing that it is I and no other who have brought this death upon you."

"Fret not, my brother," answered Owen, "for this and other things you did in the days of your blindness, and it was permitted that you should do them to an end. Kneel down now, that I may absolve you from your sins before I pass away; for I tell you, Hokosa, I believe that ere many days are over you must walk on the same path which I travel to-night."

"Is it so?" Hokosa answered. "Well, I am glad, for I have no longer any lust of life."

Then he knelt down and received the absolution.

Now John returned and Nodwengo with him, who told him that the people were gathering in hundreds according to his wish.

"Then clothe me in my robes and let us go forth," he said, "for I would speak my last words in the ears of men."

So they put the surplice and hood upon his wasted form and went out, John preceding him holding on high the ivory crucifix, while the king and Hokosa supported him, one on either side.

Without his gate stood a low wooden platform, whence at times Owen had been accustomed to address any congregation larger than the church would contain. On this platform he took his seat. The moon was bright above him, and by it he could see that already his audience numbered some thousands of men, women and children. The news had spread that the wonderful white man, Messenger, wished to take his farewell of the nation, though even now many did not understand that he was dying, but imagined that he was about to leave the country, or, for aught they knew, to vanish from their sight into Heaven. For a moment Owen looked at the sea of dusky faces, then in the midst of an intense stillness, he spoke in a voice low indeed but clear and steady:—

"My children," he said, "hear my last words to you. More than three years ago, in a far, far land and upon such a night as this, a Voice spoke to me from above commanding me to seek you out, to turn you from your idolatry and to lighten your darkness. I listened to the Voice, and hither I journeyed across sea and land, though how this thing might be done I could not guess. But to Him Who sent me all things are possible, and while yet I lingered upon the threshold of your country, in a dream were revealed to me events that were to come. So I appeared before you boldly, and knowing that he had been poisoned and that I could cure him, I drew back your king from the mouth of death, and you said to yourselves: 'Behold a wizard indeed! Let us hear him.' Then I gave battle to your sorcerers yonder upon the plain, and from the foot of the Cross I teach, the lightnings were rolled back upon them and they were not. Look now, their chief stands at my side, among my disciples one of the foremost and most faithful. Afterwards troubles arose: your king died a Christian, and many of the people fell away; but still a remnant remained, and he who became king was converted to the truth. Now I have sown the seed, and the corn is ripe before my eyes, but it is not permitted that I should reap the harvest. My work is ended, my task is done, and I, the Messenger, return to make report to Him Who sent the message.

"Hear me yet a little while, for soon shall my voice be silent. 'I come not to bring peace, but a sword,'— so said the Master Whom I preach, and so say I, the most unworthy of His servants. Salvation cannot be bought at a little price; it must be paid for by the blood and griefs of men, and in blood and griefs must you pay, O my children. Through much tribulation must you also enter the kingdom of God. Even now the heathen is at your gates, and many of you shall perish on his spears, but I tell you that he shall not conquer. Be faithful, cling to the Cross, and do not dare to doubt your Lord, for He will be your Captain and you shall be His people. Cleave to your king, for he is good; and in the day of trial listen to the counsel of this Hokosa who once was the first of evil-doers, for with him goes my spirit, and he is my son in the spirit.

"My children, fare you well! Forget me not, for I have loved you; or if you will, forget me, but remember my teaching and hearken to those who shall tread upon the path I made. The peace of God be with you, the blessing of God be upon you, and the salvation of God await you, as it awaits me to-night! Friends, lead me hence to die."

They turned to him, but before their hands touched him Thomas Owen fell forward upon the breast of Hokosa and lay there a while. Then suddenly, for the last time, he lifted himself and cried aloud:—

"I have fought a good fight! I have finished my course! I have kept the faith! Henceforth there is laid up for me a crown of righteousness . . . and not to me only, but to all those who love His appearing."

Then his head fell back, his dark eyes closed, and the Messenger was dead.

Hokosa, the man who had murdered him, having lifted him up to show him to the people, amidst a sound of mighty weeping, took the body in his arms and bore it thence to make it ready for burial.

CHAPTER XIX

THE FALL OF THE GREAT PLACE

On the morrow at sundown all that remained of Thomas Owen was laid to rest before the altar of the little church, Nodwengo the king and Hokosa lowering him into the grave, while John, his first disciple, read over him the burial service of the Christians, which it had been one of the dead man's last labours to translate into the language of the Amasuka.

Before the ceremony was finished, a soldier, carrying a spear in his hand, pushed his way through the dense and weeping crowd, and having saluted, whispered something into the ear of the king. Nodwengo started, and, with a last look of farewell at the face of his friend, left the chapel, accompanied by some of his generals who were present, muttering to Hokosa that he was to follow when all was done. Accordingly, some few minutes later, he went and was admitted into the Council Hut, where captains and messengers were to be seen arriving and departing continuously.

"Hokosa," said the king, "you have dealt treacherously with me in the past, but I believe now that your heart is true; at the least I follow the commands of our dead master and trust you. Listen: the outposts have sighted an impi of many regiments advancing towards the Great Place, though whether or no it be my own impi returning victorious from the war with my brother, I cannot say. There is this against it, however, that a messenger has but just arrived reporting that the generals have perceived the host of Hafela encamped upon a ridge over against the gorge where they awaited him. If that be so, they can scarcely have given him battle, for the messenger is swift of foot and has travelled night and day. Yet how can this be the impi of Hafela, who, say the generals, is encamped upon the ridge?"

"He may have left the ridge, King, having been warned of the ambush."

"It cannot be, for when the runner started his fires burned there and his soldiers were gathered round them."

"Then perhaps his captains sit upon the ridge with some portion of his strength to deceive those who await him in the gorge; while, knowing that here men are few, he himself swoops down on you with the main body of his impi."

"At least we shall learn presently," answered the king; "but if it be as I fear and we are outwitted, what is there that we can do against so many?"

Now one of the captains proposed that they should stay where they were and hold the place.

"It is too large," answered the king, "they will burst the fences and break our line."

Another suggested that they should fly and, avoiding the regiments of Hafela in the darkness of the night, should travel swiftly in search of the main army that had been sent to lie in ambush.

"What," said Nodwengo, "leaving the aged and the women and children to perish, for how can we take such a multitude? No, I will have none of this plan."

Then Hokosa spoke. "King," he said, "listen to my counsel: Command now that all the women and the old men, taking with them such cattle and food as are in the town, depart at once into the Valley of Death and collect in the open space that lies beyond the Tree of Doom, near the spring of water that is there. The valley is narrow and the cliffs are steep, and it may chance that by the help of Heaven we shall be able to hold it till the army returns to relieve us, to seek which messengers must be sent at once with these tidings."

"The plan is good," said the king, though none had thought of it; "but so we shall lose the town."

"Towns can be rebuilt," answered Hokosa, "but who may restore the lives of men?"

As the words left his lips, a runner burst into the council, crying: "King, the impi is that of Hafela, and the prince heads it in person. Already his outposts rest upon the Plain of Fire."

Then Nodwengo rose and issued his orders, commanding that all the ineffective population of the town, together with such food and cattle as could be gathered, should retreat at once into the Valley of Death. By this time the four or five thousand soldiers who were left in the Great Place had been paraded on the open ground in front of the king's house, where they stood, still and silent, in the moonlight. Nodwengo and the captains went out to them, and as they saw him come they lifted their spears like one man, giving him the royal salute of "King!" He held up his hand and addressed them.

"Soldiers," he said, "we have been outwitted. My impi is afar, and that of Hafela is at our gates. Yonder in the valley, though we be few, we can defend ourselves till succour reaches us, which already messengers have gone out to seek. But first we must give time for the women and children, the sick and the aged, to withdraw with food and cattle; and this we can do in one way only, by keeping Hafela at bay till they have passed the archway, all of them. Now, soldiers, for the sake of your own lives, of your honour and of those you love, swear to me, in the holy Name which we have been taught to worship, that you will fight out this great fight without fear or faltering."

"We swear it in the holy Name, and by your head, King," roared the regiments.

"Then victory is already ours," answered Nodwengo. "Follow me, Children of Fire!" and shaking his great spear, he led the way towards that portion of the outer fence upon which Hafela was advancing.

By now the town behind them was a scene of almost indescribable tumult and confusion, for the companies detailed to the task were clearing the numberless huts of their occupants, and collecting women, children and oxen in thousands, preparatory to driving them into the defile. Panic had seized many of these poor creatures, who, in imagination, already saw themselves impaled upon the cruel spears of Hafela's troops, and indeed in not a few instances believed those who were urging them forward to be the enemy. Women shrieked and wrung their hands, children wailed piteously, oxen lowed, and the infirm and aged vented their grief in groans and cries to Heaven, or their ancient god, for mercy. In truth, so difficult was the task of marshalling this motley array at night, numbering as it did ten or twelve thousand souls, that a full hour went by before the mob even began to move, slowly and uncertainly, towards the place of refuge, whereof the opening was so narrow that but few of them could pass it at a time.

Meanwhile Hafela was developing the attack. Forming his great army into the shape of a wedge he raised his battle-cry and rushed down on the first line of fortifications, which he stormed without difficulty, for they were defended by a few skirmishers only. Next he attacked the second line, and carried it after heavy fighting, then hurled himself upon the weakest point of the main fence of the vast kraal. Here it was that the fray began in earnest, for here Nodwengo was waiting for him. Thrice the thousands rolled on in the face of a storm of spears, and thrice they fell back from the wide fence of thorns and the wall of stone behind it. By now the battle had raged for about an hour and a half, and it was reported to the king that the first of the women and children had passed the archway into the valley, and that nearly all of them were clear of the eastern gate of the town.

"Then it is time that we follow them," said the king, "for if we wait here until the warriors of Hafela are among us, our retreat will become a rout and soon there will be none left to follow. Let one company," and he named it, "hold the fence for a while to give us time to withdraw, taking the wounded with us."

"We hear you, king," said one of that company, "but our captain is killed."

"Who among you will take over the command of these men and hold the breach?" asked Nodwengo of the group of officers about him.

"I, King," answered old Hokosa, lifting his spear, "for I care not whether I live or die."

"Go to, boaster!" cried another. "Who among us cares whether he lives or dies when the king commands?"

"That we shall know to-morrow," said Hokosa quietly, and the soldiers laughed at the retort.

"So be it," said the king, and while silently and swiftly he led off the regiments, keeping in the shadow of the huts, Hokosa and his hundred men posted themselves behind the weakened fence and wall. Now, for the fourth time the attacking regiment came forward grimly, on this occasion led by the prince himself. As they drew near, Hokosa leapt upon the wall, and standing there in the bright moonlight where all could see him, he called to them to halt. Instinctively they obeyed him.

"Is it Hafela whom I see yonder?" he asked.

"Ah! it is I," answered the prince. "What would you with me, wizard and traitor?"

"This only, Hafela: I would ask you what you seek here?"

"That which you promised me, Hokosa, the crown of my father and certain other things."

"Then get you back, Hafela, for you shall never win them.. Have I prophesied falsely to you at any time? Not so—neither do I prophesy falsely now. Get you back whence you came, and your wolves with you, else shall you bide here for ever."

"Do you dare to call down evil on me, Wizard?" shouted the prince furiously. "Your wife is mine, and now I take your life also," and with all his strength he hurled at him the great spear he held.

It hissed past Hokosa's head, touching his ear, but he never flinched from the steel.

"A poor cast, Prince," he said laughing; "but so it must have been, for I am guarded by that which you cannot see. My wife you have, and she shall be your ruin; my life you may take, but ere it leaves me, Hafela, I shall see you dead and your army scattered. The Messenger is passed away, but his power has fallen upon me and I speak the truth to you, O Prince and warriors, who are—already dead."

Now a shriek of dismay and fury rose from the hundreds who heard this prophesy of ill, for of Hokosa and his magic they were terribly afraid.

"Kill him! Kill the wizard!" they shouted, and a rain of spears rushed towards him on the wall.

They rushed towards him, they passed above, below, around; but, of them all, not one touched him.

"Did I not tell you that I was guarded by That which you cannot see?" Hokosa asked contemptuously. Then slowly he descended from the wall amidst a great silence.

"When men are scarce the tongue must play a part," he explained to his companions, who stared at him wondering. "By now the king and those with him should have reached the eastern gate; whereas, had we fought at once, Hafela would be hard upon his heels, for we are few, and who can hold a buffalo with a rope of grass? Yet I think that I spoke truth when I told him that the garment of the Messenger has fallen upon my shoulders, and that death awaits him and his companions, as it awaits me also and many of us. Now, friends, be ready, for the bull charges and soon we must feel his horns. This at least is left to you, to die gloriously."

While he was still speaking the first files of the regiment rushed upon the fence, tearing aside the thorns with their hands till a passage was made through them. Then they sprang upon the wall, there to be met by the spears of Hokosa and his men thrusting upward from beneath its shelter. Time after time they sprang, and time after time they fell back dead or wounded, till at last, dashing forward in one dense column, they poured over the stones as the rising tide pours over the rocks on the sea-shore, driving the defenders before them by the sheer weight of numbers.

"This game is played!" cried Hokosa. "Fly now to the eastern gate, for here we can do nothing more."

So they fled, those who survived of them, and after them came the thousands of the foe, sacking and firing the deserted town as they advanced.

Hokosa and his men, or rather the half of them, reached the gate and passed it in safety, barring it after them, and thereby delaying the attackers till they could burst their way through. Now hundreds of huts were afire, and the flames spread swiftly, lighting up the country far and wide. In the glare of them, Hokosa could see that already a full two-thirds of the crowd of fugitives had passed the narrow arch; while Nodwengo and the soldiers were drawn up in companies upon the steep and rocky slope that led to it, protecting their retreat.

He advanced to the king and reported himself.

"So you have lived through it," said Nodwengo.

"I shall die when my hour comes, and not before," Hokosa answered. "We did well yonder, and yet the most of us are alive to tell the tale, for I knew when and how to go. Be ready, king, for the foe press us close, and that mob behind us crawls onward like a snail."

As he spoke the pursuers broke through the fence and gate of the burning town, and once more the fight began. They had the advantage of numbers; but Nodwengo and his troops stood in a wide road upon higher ground protected on either side by walls, and were, moreover, rested, not breathless and weary with travel like the men of Hafela. Slowly, fighting, every inch of the way, Nodwengo was pushed back, and slowly the long ant-like line of women and sick and cattle crept through the opening in the rock, till at length all of them were gone.

"It is time," said Nodwengo, glancing behind him, "for our arms grow weary."

Then he gave orders, and company by company the defending force followed on the path of the fugitives, till at length amidst a roar of rage and disappointment, the last of them vanished through the arch, Hokosa among them, and the place was blocked with stones, above which shone a hedge of spears.

CHAPTER XX

NOMA SETS A SNARE

Thus ended the first night's battle, since for this time the enemy had fought enough. Nodwengo and his men had also had enough, for out of the five thousand of them some eleven hundred were killed or wounded. Yet they might not rest, for all that night, assisted by the women, they laboured, building stone walls across the narrowest parts of the valley. Also the cattle, women and children were moved along the gorge, which in shape may be compared to a bottle with two necks, one at either end, and encamped in the opening of the second neck, where was the spring of water. This spot was chosen both because here alone water could be obtained, without which they could not hold out more than a single day, and because the koppie whereon grew the strange-looking euphorbia known as the Tree of Doom afforded a natural rampart against attack.

Shortly after dawn, while the soldiers were resting and eating of such food as could be procured—for the most part strips of raw or half-cooked meat cut from hastily killed cattle—the onslaught was renewed with vigour, Hafela directing his efforts to the forcing of the natural archway. But, strive as he would, this he could not do, for it was choked with stones and thorns and guarded by brave men.

"You do but waste your labour, Hafela," said Noma, who stood by him watching the assault.

"What then is to be done?" he asked, "for unless we come at them we cannot kill them. It was clever of them to take refuge in this hole. I thought surely that they would fight it out yonder, beneath the fences of the Great Place."

"Ah!" she answered, "you forgot that they had Hokosa on their side. Did you then think to catch him sleeping? This retreat was Hokosa's counsel. I learned it from the lips of that wounded captain before they killed him. Now, it seems that there are but two paths to follow, and you can choose between them. The one is to send a regiment a day and a half's journey across the cliff top to guard the further mouth of the valley and to wait till these jackals starve in their hole, for certainly they can never come out."

"It has started six hours since," said Hafela, "and though the precipices are steep, having the moon to travel by, it should reach the river mouth of the valley before dawn to-morrow, cutting Nodwengo off from the plains, if indeed he should dare to venture out upon them, which, with so small a force, he will not do. Yet this first plan of yours must fail, Noma, seeing that before they starve within, the generals of Nodwengo will be back upon us from the mountains, catching us between the hammer and the anvil, and I know not how that fight would go."

"Yet, soon or late, it must be fought."

"Nay," he answered, "for my hope is that should the impi return to find Nodwengo dead, they will surrender and acknowledge me as king, who am the first of the blood royal. But what is your second plan?"

By way of answer, she pointed to the cliff above them. On the right-hand side, facing the archway, was a flat ledge overhanging the valley, at a height of about a hundred feet.

"If you can come yonder," she said, "it will be easy to storm this gate, for there lie rocks in plenty, and men cannot fight when stones are dropping on their heads."

"But how can we come to that home of vultures, where never man has set a foot? Look, the cliff above is sheer; no rock-rabbit could stand upon it."

With her eye Noma measured the distance from the brink of the precipice to the broad ledge commanding the valley.

"Sixty paces, not more," she said. "Well, yonder are oxen in plenty, and out of their hides ropes can be made, and out of ropes a ladder, down which men may pass; ten, or even five, would be enough."

"Well thought of Noma," said Hafela. "Hokosa told us last night that to him had passed the wisdom of the Messenger; but if this be so, I think that to you has passed the guile of Hokosa."

"It seems to me that some of it abides with him," answered Noma laughing.

Then the prince gave orders, and, with many workers of hides toiling at it, within two hours the ladder was ready, its staves, set twenty inches apart, being formed of knob-kerries, or the broken shafts of stabbing spears. Now they lowered it from the top of the precipice so that its end rested upon the ledge, and down it came several men, who swung upon its giddy length like spiders on a web. Reaching this great shelf in safety and advancing to the edge of it, these men started a boulder, which, although as it chanced it hurt no one, fell in the midst of a group of the defenders and bounded away through them.

"Now we must be going," said Hokosa, looking up, "for no man can fight against rocks, and our spears cannot reach those birds. Had the army been taught the use of the bow, as I counselled in the past days, we might still have held the archway; but they called it a woman's weapon, and would have none of it."

As he spoke another stone fell, crushing the life out of a man who stood next to him. Then they retreated to the first wall, which had been piled up during the night, where it was not possible to roll rocks upon them from the cliffs above. This wall, and others reared at intervals behind it, they set to work to strengthen as much as they could, making the most of the time that was left to them before the enemy could clear the way and march on to attack.

Presently Hafela's men were through and sweeping down upon them with a roar, thinking to carry the wall at a single rush. But in this they failed; indeed, it as only after an hour's hard fighting and by the expedient of continually attacking the work with fresh companies that at length they stormed the wall.

When Hokosa saw that he could no longer hold the place, but before the foe was upon him, he drew off his soldiers to the second wall, a quarter of a mile or more away, and here the fight began again. And so it went on for hour after hour, as one by one the fortifications were carried by the weight of numbers, for the attackers fought desperately under the eye of their prince, caring nothing for the terrible loss they suffered in men. Twice the force of the defenders was changed by order of Nodwengo, fresh men being sent from the companies held in reserve to take the places of those who had borne the brunt of the battle. This indeed it was necessary to do, seeing that it was impossible to carry water to so many, and in that burning valley men could not fight for long athirst. Only Hokosa stayed on, for they brought him drink in a gourd, and wherever the fray was fiercest there he was always; nor although spears were rained upon him by hundreds, was he touched by one of them.

At length as the night fell the king's men were driven back from their last scherm in the western half of the valley, across the open space back upon the koppie where stood the Tree of Doom. Here they stayed a while till, overmatched and outworn, they were pushed from its rocks across the narrow stretch of broken ground into the shelter of the great stone scherm or wall that ran from side to side of the further neck of the valley, whereon thousands of women and such men as could be spared had been working incessantly during the past night and day.

It was as he retreated among the last upon this wall that Hokosa caught sight of Noma for the first time since they parted in the house of the Messenger. In the forefront of his troops, directing the attack, was Hafela the prince, and at his side stood Noma, carrying in her hand a little shield and a spear. At this moment also she saw him and called aloud to him:—

"You have fought well, Wizard, but to-morrow all your magic shall avail you nothing, for it will be your last day upon this earth."

"Ay, Noma," he answered, "and yours also."

Then of a sudden a company of the king's men rushed from the shelter of the wall upon the attackers driving them back to the koppie and killing several, so that in the confusion and gathering darkness Hokosa lost sight of her, though a man at his side declared that he saw her fall beneath the thrust of an assegai. Thus ended the second day.

Now when the watch had been set the king and his captains took counsel together, for their hearts were heavy.

"Listen," said Nodwengo: "out of five thousand soldiers a thousand have been killed and a thousand lie among us wounded. Hark to the groaning of them! Also we have with us women and children and sick to the number of twelve thousand, and between us and those who would butcher them every one there stands but a single wall. Nor is this the worst of it: the spring cannot supply the wants of so great a multitude in this hot place, and it is feared that presently the water will be done. What way shall we turn? If we surrender to Hafela, perhaps he will spare the lives of the women and children; but whatever he may promise, the most of us he will surely slay. If we fight and are defeated, then once his regiments are among us, all will be slain according to the ancient custom of our people. I have bethought me that we might retreat through the valley, but the river beyond is in flood; also it is certain that before this multitude could reach it, the prince will have sent a force to cut us off while he himself harasses our rear. Now let him who has counsel speak."

"King, I have counsel," said Hokosa. "What were the words that the Messenger spoke to us before he died? Did he not say: 'Even now the heathen is at your gates, and many of you shall perish on his spears; but I tell you that he shall not conquer'? Did he not say: 'Be faithful, cling to the Cross, and do not dare to doubt your Lord, for He will protect you, and your children after you, and He will be your Captain and you shall be His people'? Did he not bid you also to listen to my counsel? Then listen to it, for it is his: Your case seems desperate, but have no fear, and take no thought for the morrow, for all shall yet be well. Let us now pray to Him that the Messenger has revealed to us, and Whom now he implores on our behalf in that place where he is to guide us and to save us, for then surely He will hearken to our prayer."

"So be it," said Nodwengo, and going out he stood upon a pillar of stone in the moonlight and offered up his supplication in the hearing of the multitude.

Meanwhile, those of the camp of Hafela were also taking counsel. They had fought bravely indeed, and carried the schanses; but at great cost, since for every man that Nodwengo had lost, three of theirs had fallen. Moreover, they were in evil case with weariness and the want of water, as each drop they drank must be carried to them from the Great Place in bags made of raw hide, which caused it to stink, for they had but few gourds with them.

"Now it is strange," said Hafela, "that these men should fight so bravely, seeing that they are but a handful. There can be scarce three thousand of them left, and yet I doubt not that before we carry those last walls of theirs as many of us or more will be done. Ay! and after they are done with, we must meet their great impi when it returns, and of what will befall us then I scarcely like to think."

"Ill-fortune will befall you while Hokosa lives," broke in Noma. "Had it not been for him, this trouble would have been done with by now; but he is a wizard, and by his wizardries he defeats us and puts heart into Nodwengo and the warriors. You, yourself, have seen him this day defying us, not once but many times, for upon his flesh steel has no power. Ay! and this is but the beginning of evil, for I am sure that he leads you into some deep trap where you shall perish everlastingly. Did he not himself declare that the power of that dead white worker of miracles has fallen upon him, and who can fight against magic?"

"Who, indeed?" said Hafela humbly; for like all savages he was very superstitious, and, moreover, a sincere believer in Hokosa's supernatural capacities. "This wizard is too strong for us; he is invulnerable, and as I know well he can read the secret thoughts of men and can suck wisdom from the dead, while to his eyes the darkness is no blind."

"Nay, Hafela," answered Noma, "there is one crack in his shield. Hear me: if we can but catch him and hold him fast we shall have no need to fear him more, and I think that I know how to bait the trap."

"How will you bait it?" asked Hafela.

"Thus. Midway between the koppie and the wall behind which lie the men of the king stands a flat rock, and all about that rock are stretched the bodies of dead soldiers. Now, this is my plan: that when next one of those dark storm-clouds passes over the face of the moon six of the strongest of our warriors should creep upon their bellies down this way and that, as though they were also numbered with the slain. This done, you shall despatch a herald to call in the ears of the king that you desire to treat with him of peace. Then he will answer that if this be so you can come beneath the walls of his camp, and your herald shall refuse, saying that you fear treachery. But he must add that if Nodwengo will bid Hokosa to advance alone to the flat rock, you will bid me, Noma, whom none can fear, to do likewise, and that there we can talk in sight of both armies, and returning thence, make report to you and to Nodwengo. Afterwards, so soon as Hokosa has set his foot upon the rock, those men who seem to be dead shall spring upon him and drag him to our camp, where we can deal with him; for once the wizard is taken, the cause of Nodwengo is lost."

"A good pitfall," said the prince; "but will Hokosa walk into the trap?"

"I think so, Hafela, for three reasons. He is altogether without fear; he will desire, if may be, to make peace on behalf of the king; and he has this strange weakness, that he still loves me, and will scarcely suffer an occasion of speaking with me to go past, although he has divorced me."

"So be it," said the prince; "the game can be tried, and if it fails, why we lose nothing, whereas if it succeeds we gain Hokosa, which is much; for with you I think that our arms will never prosper while that accursed wizard sits yonder weaving his spells against us, and bringing our men to death by hundreds and by thousands."

Then he gave his orders, and presently, when a cloud passed over the face of the moon, six chosen men crept forward under the lee of the flat rock and threw themselves down here and there amongst the dead.

Soon the cloud passed, and the herald advanced across the open space blowing a horn, and waving a branch in his hand to show that he came upon a mission of peace.

CHAPTER XXI

HOKOSA IS LIFTED UP

"What would you?" asked Hokosa of the herald as he halted a short spear-cast from the wall.

"My master, the Prince Hafela, desires to treat with your master, Nodwengo. Many men have fallen on either side, and if this war goes on, though victory must be his at last, many more will fall. Therefore, if any plan can be found, he desires to spare their lives."

Now Hokosa spoke with the king, and answered:—

"Then let Hafela come beneath the wall and we will talk with him."

"Not so," answered the herald. "Does a buck walk into an open pit? Were the prince to come here it might chance that your spears would talk with him. Let Nodwengo follow me to the camp yonder, where we promise him safe conduct."

"Not so," answered Hokosa. "'Does a buck walk into an open pit?' Set out your message, and we will consider it."

"Nay, I am but a common man without authority; but I am charged to make you another offer, and if you will not hear it then there is an end. Let Hokosa advance alone to that flat rock you see yonder, and there he shall be met, also alone, by one having power to talk with him, namely, by the Lady Noma, who was once his wife. Thus they can confer together midway between the camps and in full sight of both of them, nor, no man being near, can he find cause to be afraid of an unarmed girl. What say you?"

Hokosa turned and talked with the king.

"I think it well that you should not go," said Nodwengo. "The offer seems fair, and the stone is out of reach of their spears; still, behind it may lurk a scheme to kill or capture you, for Hafela is very cunning."

"It may be so, King," answered Hokosa; "still, my heart tells me it is wisest that I should do this thing, for our case is desperate, and if I do it not, that may be the cause of the death of all of us to-morrow. At the worst, I am but one man, and it matters little what may chance to me; nor shall I come to any harm unless it is the will of Heaven that it should be so; and be sure of this, that out of the harm will arise good, for where I go there the spirit of the Messenger goes with me. Remember that he bade you listen to my counsel while I remain with you, seeing that I do not speak of my own wisdom. Therefore let me go, and if it should chance that I am taken, trouble not about the matter, for thus it will be fated to some great end. Above all, though often enough I have been a traitor in the past, do not dream that I betray you, keeping in mind that so to do would be to betray my own soul, which very soon must render its account on high."

"As you will, Hokosa," answered the king. "And now tell those rebel dogs that on these terms only will I make peace with them—that they withdraw across the mountains by the path which their women and children have taken, leaving this land for ever without lifting another spear against us. If they will do this, notwithstanding all the wickedness and slaughter that they have worked, I will send command to my impi to let them go unharmed. If they will not do this, I put my trust in the God I worship and will fight this fray out to the end, knowing that if I and my people perish, they shall perish also."

Now Nodwengo himself spoke to the herald who was waiting beyond the wall.

"Go back to him you serve," he said, "and say that Hokosa will meet her who was his wife upon the flat stone and talk with her in the sight of both armies, bearing my word with him. At the sound of the blowing of a horn shall each of them advance unarmed and alone from either camp. Say to my brother also that it will indeed be ill for him if he attempts treachery upon Hokosa, for the man who causes his blood to flow will surely die, and after death shall be accursed for ever."

The herald went, and presently a horn was blown.

"Now it comes into my mind that we part for the last time," said Nodwengo in a troubled voice as he took the hand of Hokosa.

"It may be so, King; in my heart I think that it is so; yet I do not altogether grieve thereat, for the burden of my past sins crushes me, and I am weary and seek for rest. Yet we do not part for the last time, because whatever chances, in the end I shall make my report to you yonder"—and he pointed upwards. "Reign on for long years, King—reign well and wisely, clinging to the Faith, for thus at the last shall you reap your reward. Farewell!"

Now again the horn blew, and in the bright moonlight the slight figure of Noma could be seen advancing towards the stone.

Then Hokosa sprang from the wall and advanced also, till at the same moment they climbed upon the stone.

"Greeting, Hokosa," said Noma, and she stretched out her hand to him.

By way of answer he placed his own behind his back, saying: "To your business, woman." Yet his eyes searched her face—the face which in his folly he still loved; and thus it came about that he never saw sundry of the dead bodies, which lay in the shadow of the stone, begin to quicken into life, and inch by inch to arise, first to their knees and next to their feet. He never saw or heard them, yet, as the words left his lips, they sprang upon him from every side, holding him so that he could not move.

"Away with him!" cried Noma with a laugh of triumph; and at her command he was half-dragged and half-carried across the open space and thrust violently over a stone wall into the camp of Hafela.

Now Nodwengo and his soldiers saw what had happened, and with a shout of "Treachery!" some hundreds of them leapt into the plain and began to run towards the koppie to rescue their envoy.

Hokosa heard the shout, and wrenching himself round, beheld them.

"Back!" he cried in a clear, shrill voice. "Back! children of Nodwengo, and leave me to my fate, for the foe waits for you by thousands behind the wall!"

A soldier struck him across the mouth, bidding him be silent; but his warning had come to the ears of Nodwengo, causing him and his warriors to halt and begin a retreat. It was well that they did so, for seeing that they would not come on, from under the shelter of the wall and of every rock and stone soldiers jumped up by companies and charged, driving them back to their own schanse. But the king's men had the start of them, and had taken shelter behind it, whence they greeted them with a volley of spears, killing ten and wounding twice as many more.

Now it was Hokosa's turn to laugh, and laugh he did, saying:—

"My taking is well paid for already, Prince. A score of your best warriors is a heavy price to give for the carcase of one weary and aging man. But since I am here among you, captured with so much pain and loss, tell me of your courtesy why I have been brought."

Then the prince shook his spear at him and cursed him.

"Would you learn, wizard and traitor?" he cried. "We have caught you because we know well that while you stay yonder your magic counsel will prevail against our might; whereas, when once we hold you fast, Nodwengo will wander to his ruin like a blind and moonstruck man, for you were to him both eyes and brain."

"I understand," said Hokosa calmly. "But, Prince, how if I left my wisdom behind me?"

"That may not be," answered Hafela, "since even a wizard cannot throw his thoughts into the heart of another from afar."

"Ah! you think so, Prince. Well, ask Noma yonder if I cannot throw my thoughts into her heart from afar: though of late I have not chosen to do so, having put aside such spells. But let it pass, and tell me, having taken me, what is it you propose to do with me? First, however, I will give you for nothing some of that wisdom which you grudge to Nodwengo the king. Be advised by me, Prince, and take the terms that he offers to you—namely, to turn this very night and begone from the land without harm or hindrance. Will you receive my gift, Hafela?"

"What will happen if I refuse it?" asked the prince slowly.

Now Hokosa looked at the dust at his feet, then he gazed upwards searching the heavens, and answered:—

"Did not I tell you yesterday? I think that this will happen. I think—but who can be quite sure of the future, Hafela?—that you and the most of your army by this hour to-morrow night will be lying fast asleep about this place, with jackals for your bedfellows."

The prince heard and trembled at his words, for he believed that if he willed it, Hokosa could prophesy the truth.

"Accursed dog!" he said. "I am minded to be guided by your saying; but be sure of this, that if I follow it, you shall stay here to sleep with jackals, yes, this very night."

Then Noma broke in.

"Be not mad, Hafela!" she said. "Will you listen to the lies that this renegade tells to work upon your fears? Will you abandon victory when it lies within your grasp, and in place of a great king become a fugitive whom all men mock at, an outcast to be hunted down at leisure by that brother against whom you dared to rebel, but on whom you did not dare to shut your hand when he lay in its hollow? Silence the tongue of this captive rogue for ever and become a man again, with the heart of a man."

"Now," said Hokosa gently; "many would find it hard to believe that I reared this woman from childhood, nursing her with my own hands when she was sick and giving her of the best I had; that afterwards, when you stole her from me, Prince, I sinned deeply to win her back. That I married her and sinned yet more deeply to give her the greatness she desired; and at last, of my own will, I loosed the bonds by which I held her, although I could not thrust her memory from my heart. Yet I have earned it all, for I made her the tool of my witchcraft, and therefore it is just that she should turn and rend me. Well, if you like it, take her counsel, Prince, and let mine go, for I care nothing which you take; only, forgive me if I prophesy once more and for the last time—I am sure that Nodwengo yonder spoke truth when he bade your herald tell me that he who causes my blood to flow shall surely die and for it be called to a strict account. Prince, I am a Christian now, and believe me, whatever you may do, I seek no revenge upon you; having been myself forgiven so much, in my turn I have learned to forgive. Yet it may be ill for that man who causes my blood to flow."

"Let him be strangled," said a captain who stood near by, "and then there will be no blood in the matter."

"Friend," answered Hokosa, "you should have been not a soldier but a pleader of causes. True it is then that the prince will only cause my life to fly, but whether that is a smaller sin I leave you to judge."

"Keep him prisoner," said another, "till we learn how these matters end."

"Nay," answered Hafela, "for then he will surely outwit us and escape. Noma, what shall we do with this man who was your husband? Tell us, for you should know best how to deal with him."

"Let me think," she answered, and she looked first at the ground beneath her, next around her, then upwards toward the skies.

Now they stood at the foot of the koppie, on the flat top of which grew the great Tree of Doom, that for generations had served the People of Fire as a place of execution of their criminals, or of those who fell under the ban of the king or of the witch-doctors. Among and above the finger-like fronds of this strange and dreadful-looking tree towered that white dead limb shaped like a cross, which Owen had pointed out to his disciple John, taking it to be a sign and a promise. This cross stood out clear against the sinking moon. It caught Noma's eye, and a devilish thought entered into her heart.

"You would keep this fellow alive?" she said, "and yet you would not suffer him to escape. See, there above you is a cross such as he worships. Bind him to it as he says the Man whom he worships was bound, and let that dead Man help him if he may."

The prince and those about Noma shrank back a little in horror. They were cruel men rendered more cruel by their superstitious fear of one whom they believed to be uncanny; one to whom they attributed inhuman powers which he was exercising to their destruction, but still this doom seemed dreadful to them. Noma read their minds and went on passionately:—

"You deem me unmerciful, but you do not know what I have suffered at this wizard's hands. For his sake and because of him I am haunted. For his own purposes he opened the gates of Distance, he sent me down among the dwellers in Death, causing me to interpret their words for him. I did so, but the dwellers came back out of Death with me, and from that hour they have not left me, nor will they ever leave me; for night by night they sojourn at my side, tormenting me with terrors. He has told me that through my mouth that spirit whom he drew into my body prophesied that he should be 'lifted up above the people.' Let the prophecy be fulfilled, let him be lifted up, for then perchance the ghosts will depart from me and I shall win peace and sleep. Also, thus alone can you hold him safe and yet shed no blood."

"Be it so," said the prince. "When we plotted together of the death of the king, and as your price, Hokosa, you bargained for the girl whom I had chosen to wife, did I not warn you that this witch of many spells, who holds both our hearts in her little hands, should yet hound you to death and mock you while you perished by an end of shame? What did I tell you, Hokosa?"

Now when he heard his fate, Hokosa bowed his head and trembled a little. Then he lifted it, and exclaimed in a clear voice:—

"It is true, Prince, but I will add to your words. She shall bring both of us to death. For me, I am honoured indeed in that there has been allotted to me that same end which my Master chose. To that cross let my sins be fastened and with them my body."

Now the moon sank, but in the darkness men were found who dared to climb the tree, taking with them strips of raw hide. They reached the top of it, four of them, and seating themselves upon the arms of the cross, they let down a rope, the noose of which was placed about the body of Hokosa. As it tightened upon him, he turned his calm and dreadful eyes on to the eyes of Noma and said to her:—

"Woman, I do not reproach you; but I lay this fate upon you, that you shall watch me die. Thereafter, let God deal with you as He may choose."

Now, when she heard these words Noma shrieked aloud, for of a sudden she felt that the power of the will of Hokosa, from which she had been freed by him, had once more fallen upon her, and that come what might she was doomed to obey his last commands.

Little by little the soldiers drew him up and in the darkness they bound him fast there upon the lofty cross. Then they descended and left him, and would have led Noma with them from the tree. But this they could not do, for always she broke from them screaming, and fled back to its shadow.

Then, seeing that she was bewitched, Hafela commanded that they should bind a cloth about her mouth and leave her there till her senses returned to her in the sunlight—for none of them dared to stop with her in the shadow of that tree, since the odours of it were poisonous to man. Also they believed the place to be haunted by evil spirits.

CHAPTER XXII

THE VICTORY OF THE CROSS

The sun rose suddenly over the edge of the cliffs, and while it was yet deep shadow in the valley, its red light struck upon the white cross of perished wood that towered above the Tree of Doom and on the black shape of Hokosa crucified to it living. The camp of the king saw and understood, and from every throat of the thousands of men, women and children gathered there, went up a roar of rage and horror. The king lifted his hand, and silence fell upon the place; then he mounted on the wall and cried aloud:—

"Do you yet live, Hokosa, or is it your body only that those traitors have fastened to the tree?"

Back came the answer through the clear still air:—

"I live, O King!"

"Endure then a little while," called Nodwengo, "and we will storm the tree and save you."

"Nay," answered Hokosa, "you cannot save me; yet before I die I shall see you saved."

Then his words were lost in tumult, for the third day's fighting began. Desperately the regiments of Hafela rushing across the open space, hurled themselves upon the fortifications, which, during the night, had been strengthened by the building of two inner walls. Nor was this all, for suddenly a cry told those in front that the regiment which Hafela had despatched across the mountains had travelled up the eastern neck of the valley, and were attacking the position in their rear. Well was it for Nodwengo now that he had listened to the counsel of Hokosa, and, wearied as his soldiers were, had commanded that here also a great wall should be built.

For two hours the fight raged, and then on either side the foe fell back, not beaten indeed, though their dead were many, but to rest and take counsel. But now a new trouble arose: from all the camp of Nodwengo there went up a moan of pain to Heaven, for since the evening of yesterday the spring had given out, and they had found no water wherewith to wet their lips. During the night they bore it; but now the sun beating down on the black rocks with fearful force scorched them to the marrow, till they began to wither like fallen leaves, and already wounded men and children died, while the warriors cut the throats of oxen and drank their blood.

Hokosa hanging on his cross heard this moaning and divined its cause.

"Be of good comfort, children of Nodwengo," he cried; "for I will pray that rain be sent upon you." And he lifted his head and prayed.

Now, whether it was by chance or whether his prayer was heard, who can say? At least it happened that immediately thereafter clouds began to gather and to thicken in the blue of Heaven, and within two hours rain fell in torrents, so that every one could drink his fill, and the spring being replenished at its sources, flowed again strongly.

After the rain came cold and moaning winds, and after the wind a great gloom and thunder.

Now, taking advantage of the shadow, the regiments of Hafela renewed their attack, and this time they carried the first of the three walls, for its defenders grew feeble and few in number. There they paused a while, and save for the cries of the wounded and of frightened women, the silence was great.

"Let your hearts be filled up!" cried the voice of Hokosa through the silence; "for the sunlight shines upon the plain of the Great Place yonder, and in it I see the sheen of spears. The impi travels to your aid, O children of Nodwengo."

Now, at this tidings the people of the king shouted for joy; but Hafela called to his regiments to make an end of them, and they hurled themselves upon the second wall, fighting desperately. Again and again they were beaten back, and again and again they came on, till at length they carried this wall also, driving its defenders, or those who remained alive of them, into the third entrenchment, and paused to rest awhile.

"Pray for us, O Prophet who are set on high!" cried a voice from the camp, "for if succour do not reach us speedily, we are sped."

Before the echoes of the voice had died away, a flash of lightning flared through the gloom, and in the light of it Hokosa saw that the king's impi was rushing up the gorge.

"Fight on! Fight on!" he called in answer. "I have prayed to Heaven, and your succour is at hand."

Then, with a howl of rage, Hafela's regiments hurled themselves upon the third and last entrenchment, attacking it at once in front and rear. Twice they nearly carried it, but each time the wild scream of Hokosa on high was heard above the din, conjuring its defenders to fight on and fear not, for Heaven had sent them help. They fought as men have seldom fought before, and with them fought the women and even the children. They were few and the foe was still many, but they listened to the urging of him whom they believed to be inspired in his death-agony upon the cross above them, and still they held their own. Twice portions of the wall were torn down, but they filled the breach with the corpses of the dead, ay! and with the bodies of the living, for the wounded, the old men and the very women piled themselves there in the place of stones. No such fray was told of in the annals of the People of Fire as this, the last stand of Nodwengo against the thousands of Hafela. Now all the shouting had died away, for men had no breath left wherewith to shout, only from the gloomy place of battle came low groans and the deep sobbing sighs of warriors gripped in the death-hug.

"Fight on! Fight on!" shrilled the voice of Hokosa on high. "Lo! the skies are open to my dying sight, and I see the impis of Heaven sweeping to succour you. Behold!"

They dashed the sweat from their eyes and looked forth, and as they looked, the pall of gloom was lifted, and in the golden glow of many-shafted light, they saw, not the legions of Heaven indeed, but the regiments of Nodwengo rushing round the bend of the valley, as dogs rush upon a scent, with heads held low and spears outstretched.

Hafela saw them also.

"Back to the koppie," he cried, "there to die like men, for the wizardries of Hokosa have been too strong for us, and lost is this my last battle and the crown I came to seek!"

They obeyed, and all that were left of them, some ten thousand men, they ran to the koppie and formed themselves upon it, ring above ring, and here the soldiers of Nodwengo closed in upon them.

Again and for the last time the voice of Hokosa rang out above the fray.

"Nodwengo," he cried, "with my passing breath I charge you have mercy and spare these men, so many of them as will surrender. The day of bloodshed has gone by, the fray is finished, the Cross has conquered. Let there be peace in the land."

All men heard him, for his piercing scream, echoed from the precipices, came to the ears of each. All men heard him, and, even in that fierce hour of vengeance, all obeyed. The spear that was poised was not thrown, and the kerry lifted over the fallen did not descend to dash away his life.

"Hearken, Hafela!" called the king, stepping forward from the ranks of the attackers. "He whom you have set on high to bring defeat upon you charges me to give you peace, and in the name of the conquering Cross I give peace. All who surrender shall dwell henceforth in my shadow, nor shall the head or the heel of one of them be harmed, although their sin is great. One life only will I take, the life of that witch who brought your armies down upon me to burn my town and slay my people by thousands, and who but last night betrayed Hokosa to his death of torment. All shall go free, I say, save the witch; and for you, you shall be given cattle and such servants as will cling to you to the number of a hundred, and driven from the land. Now, what say you? Will you yield or be slain? Swift with your answer; for the sun sinks, and ere it is set there must be an end in this way or in that."

The regiments of Hafela heard, and shouted in answer as with one voice:—

"We take your mercy, King! We fought bravely while we could, and now we take your mercy, King!"

"What say you, Hafela?" repeated Nodwengo, addressing the prince, who stood upon a point of rock above him in full sight of both armies.

Hafela turned and looked at Hokosa hanging high in mid-air.

"What say I?" he answered in a slow and quiet voice. "I say that the Cross and its Prophet have been too strong for me, and that I should have done well to follow the one and to listen to the counsel of the other. My brother, you tell me that I may go free, taking servants with me. I thank you and I will go—alone."

And setting the handle of his spear upon the rock, with a sudden movement he fell forward, transfixing his heart with its broad blade, and lay still.

"At least he died like one of the blood-royal of the Sons of Fire!" cried Nodwengo, while the armies stood silent and awestruck, "and with the blood-royal he shall be buried. Lay down your arms, you who followed him and fought for him, fearing nothing, and give over to me the witch that she may be slain."

"She hides under the tree yonder!" cried a voice.

"Go up and take her," said Nodwengo to some of his captains.

Now Noma, crouched on the ground beneath the tree, had seen and heard all that passed. Perceiving the captains making their way towards her through the lines of the soldiers, who opened out a path for them, she rose and for a moment stood bewildered. Then, as though drawn by some strange attraction, she turned, and seizing hold of the creeper that clung about it, she began to climb the Tree of Doom swiftly. Up she went while all men watched, higher and higher yet, till passing out of the finger-like foliage she reached the cross of dead wood whereto Hokosa hung, and placing her feet upon one arm of it, stood there, supporting herself by the broken top of the upright.

Hokosa was not yet dead, though he was very near to death. Lifting his glazing eyes, he knew her and said, speaking thickly:—

"What do you here, Noma, and wherefore have you come?"

"I come because you draw me," she answered, "and because they seek my life below."

"Repent, repent!" he whispered, "there is yet time and Heaven is very merciful."

She heard, and a fury seized her.

"Be silent, dog!" she cried. "Having defied your God so long, shall I grovel to Him at the last? Having hated you so much, shall I seek your forgiveness now? At least of one thing I am glad—it was I who brought you here, and with me and through me you shall die."

Then, placing one foot upon his bent head as if in scorn, she leaned forward, her long hair flying to the wind, and cursed Nodwengo and his people, naming them renegades and apostates, and cursed the soldiers of Hafela, naming them cowards, calling down upon them the malison of their ancestors.

Hokosa heard and muttered:—

"For your soul's sake, woman, repent! repent, ere it be too late!"

"Repent!" she screamed, catching at his words. "Thus do I repent!" and drawing the knife from her girdle, she leant over him and drove it hilt-deep into his breast.

Then with a sudden movement she sprang upwards and outwards into the air, and rushing down through a hundred feet of space, was struck dead upon that very rock where the corpse of Hafela lay.

Now, beneath the agony of the life Hokosa lifted his head for the last time, crying in a great voice:—

"Messenger, I come, be you my guide," and with the words his soul passed.

"All is over and ended," said a voice. "Soldiers, salute the king with the royal salute."

"Nay," answered Nodwengo. "Salute me not, salute the Cross and him who hangs thereon."

So, while the rays of the setting sun shone about it, regiment by regiment that great army rushed past the koppie, and pausing opposite to the cross and its burden, they rendered to it the royal salute of kings.

Then the night fell, and thus through the power of Faith that now, as of old, is the only true and efficient magic, was accomplished the mission to the Sons of Fire of the Saint and Martyr, Thomas Owen, and of his murderer and disciple, the Wizard Hokosa.

Sir Henry Rider Haggard, KBE was born on June 22nd, 1856 at Bradenham in Norfolk, England.

More familiarly known as H. Rider Haggard, he was the eighth of ten children born to Sir William Meybohm Rider Haggard, a barrister (born, incidentally, in St Petersburg, Russia), and Ella Doveton, an author, poet and daughter of a merchant in the East India Trading Company.

Haggard was initially schooled at Garsington Rectory in Oxfordshire where he studied under the tutelage of Reverend H. J. Graham. His elder brothers, who seemed to find more favour with their father, graduated from various private schools whilst Haggard was sent to Ipswich Grammar School, saving his father a considerable sum in fees.

He failed his army entrance exam, and was therefore sent to a private crammer in London in preparation for the entrance exam to the British Foreign Office, which he appears never to have sat. However, it was during his two years in London that Haggard came into contact with a circle of people interested in the study of psychical phenomena and for which he too now developed a life-long interest together with a series of enduring friendships.

In 1875, Haggard's father used his family's connections to send him to Southern Africa to take up an unpaid position as assistant to the secretary to Sir Henry Bulwer, Lieutenant-Governor of the Colony of Natal. In 1876 he was transferred to the staff of Sir Theophilus Shepstone, Special Commissioner for the Transvaal. It was in this role that Haggard was present in Pretoria in April 1877 for the official announcement of the British annexation of the Boer Republic of the Transvaal. The official who had been nominated to read out the Proclamation lost his voice and Haggard was his replacement. It was a moment in history.

Haggard was to remain in the country for six years, during which time he served as Master of the High Court of the Transvaal and an adjutant of the Pretoria Horse.

It was here that he fell in love with Mary Elizabeth "Lilly" Jackson. He hoped to marry her once he obtained more certainty in his career path.

In 1878 he became Registrar of the High Court in the Transvaal and now the time seemed opportune to write to his father to tell him of his hope to marry. The reply from his father was uncompromising. He forbade it until his son had made a proper career for himself.

The following year, 1879, Lily married Frank Archer, a well-to-do banker.

Haggard returned briefly to England to marry a friend of his sister's, Marianna Louisa Margitson, a 21 year old, in 1880, and the couple travelled to Africa together. Haggard's years in Africa had proved, at least on a writing level, rich and inspirational for him, and while still in Natal he wrote two articles for The Gentleman's Magazine describing his experiences.

Moving back to England in (and accounts here differ as to whether it was 1881 or 1882) the couple settled in Ditchingham, Norfolk, Louisa's ancestral home. Later they moved to Kessingland and established connections with the church in Bungay, Suffolk. The marriage produced four children. A son named Jack (who tragically died at age 10 of measles) and three daughters, Angela, Dorothy and Lilias. (Lilias grew to become an author and her father's biographer.)

In England Law was to be the fulcrum of his career. However, although he studied, writing was growing in its appeal to him. His first book, Cetywayo and His White Neighbours, was an account and study of Britain's policies in South Africa.

From this point his career as a writer began to take substantial hold and with it a dramatic shift to fiction. Two years later he published his first fiction, Dawn followed in 1885 by arguably his most popular novel, King Solomon's Mines—detailing the life of the adventurer Allan Quatermain. This was followed the following year, 1886, by She: A History of Adventure, which introduced the female character Ayesha. Both characters, Quatermain and Ayesha, developed a series of books about their adventures.

The study of Law now fell away entirely. He appeared also to have a keen sense of his commercial appreciation. Rather than sell the copyright of his first best-seller, King Solomon's Mines, for a £100 fee he, instead, accepted a 10% royalty. This book is also generally accepted as the first of the Lost World writing genre.

Haggard obviously thought there were many further adventures to tell and it would be hard to find a publisher who would disagree given the start he had made. Sequels soon followed. Allan Quatermain continued his epic and swash-buckling adventures in Africa whilst the sequel to She entitled Ayesha played out her adventures in Tibet. Interestingly Haggard would later extend his characters adventures around the world with Eric Brighteyes, being the basis for an epic Viking romance.

The Haggard family lived at 69 Gunterstone Road in Hammersmith, London, from mid-1885 to mid-1888. It was here that he wrote his most famous works. His time in Africa had given him the experience and atmosphere as well as several observations and friendships of the people who would so influence his fictional characters. Chief among them were the larger-than-life adventurers Frederick Selous and Frederick Russell Burnham. Both were men of Empire and huge ambition as they helped uncover the great mineral wealth of Africa, as well as the ruins of ancient lost civilisations of the continent, such as Great Zimbabwe.

Three of Haggard's books, The Wizard (1896), Black Heart and White Heart; a Zulu Idyll (1896), and Elissa; the Doom of Zimbabwe (1898), are dedicated to Burnham's daughter Nada, the first white child born in Bulawayo; she had been named after Haggard's 1892 book Nada the Lily.

As is typical of the writing of the time his novels contain many of the stereotypes associated with colonialism, yet they also sympathise, to a degree, with the native populations. Africans often play heroic roles in the novels, although the protagonists are more often than not European. The time around the turn of the century was, after all, the great sprint to Empire by many European countries intent on gaining possessions of land, people and resources.

Three of Haggard's novels were written in collaboration with his friend Andrew Lang who shared his interest in the spiritual realm and paranormal phenomena and who was also a greatly admired editor.

Haggard's stories are still widely read today. Ayesha, the female protagonist of She, has been cited as a prototype by psychoanalysts such as Sigmund Freud (in The Interpretation of Dreams) and Carl Jung. Her epithet is, of course, "She Who Must Be Obeyed" and has for decades been used tongue-in-cheek to describe the presumed balance of influence between the sexes.

As a legacy it is easy to establish Haggard, and his pioneering work, as the author of the Lost World branch of writing and its influence of such other writers as Edgar Rice Burroughs, Robert E. Howard and Talbot Mundy. The Allan Quatermain character influenced many 'serials' in Hollywood during the 30s & 40s and can readily be seen as a template for Indiana Jones, the American archaeologist and explorer and huge box office film character.

Years later, when Haggard was a successful novelist, he was contacted by his former love, Lilly Archer, née Jackson. Lily had been deserted by her husband, who had embezzled funds and fled bankrupt to Africa. Haggard installed her and her sons in a house and saw to the children's education. Lilly eventually followed her husband to Africa, where he infected her with syphilis before dying of it himself. Lilly returned to England in late 1907, where Haggard again supported her until her death on April 22nd, 1909.

Haggard also wrote about agricultural and social reform, in part inspired by his experiences in Africa, but also based on what he saw in Europe. By the end of his life, he was adamantly opposed to Bolshevism, a position that he shared with his life-long friend Rudyard Kipling. The two had found friendship upon Kipling's arrival at London in 1889 largely on the strength of their shared opinions.

Haggard was extremely interested in the social affairs of the Country and eager to play a more active part in attempting reform. In 1895 he stood unsuccessfully for Parliament as a Conservative candidate for the Eastern division of Norfolk losing by 198 votes.

Also in 1895 he served on a government commission to examine Salvation Army labour colonies. This, and his heavy involvement in agriculture reform, led to him being a member of several further commissions on land use and related affairs, work that involved several trips to the Colonies and Dominions. This work, in part, helped lead to the passage of the 1909 Development Bill.

In 1911 he served on the Royal Commission examining coastal erosion.

He was an absorbed and dedicated writer of letters to The Times, nearly one hundred were published by them and the bibliography attached below reveals much in the range of subjects he wished to bring attention to.

He was made a Knight Bachelor in 1912 and a Knight Commander of the Order of the British Empire in 1919. Haggard was a member of several clubs including the Athenaeum, Savile, and Authors' clubs.

The district of Rider in British Columbia, Canada, was named in his honour.

Henry Rider Haggard died on May 14th, 1925 at the age of 68. His ashes were buried at Ditchingham Church. His papers are held at the Norfolk Record Office.

The first chapter of his book People of the Mist (1894) is credited with inspiring the 1912 motto of the Royal Air Force (formerly the Royal Flying Corps), Per ardua ad astra. "Through adversity to the stars" (or alternately "Through struggle to the stars") it is also used by other Commonwealth air forces such as the RAAF, RCAF, RNZAF, and the SAAF.

H. Rider Haggard – A Concise Bibliography

Novels

Dawn (1884) Published in three volumes
The Witch's Head (1884) Published in three volumes
King Solomon's Mines (1885) Allan Quatermain series
She: A History of Adventure (1886) Ayesha series
Allan Quatermain (1887) Allan Quatermain series
Jess (1887)
A Tale of Three Lions (1887) Allan Quatermain series
Maiwa's Revenge, or the War of the Little Hand (1888) Allan Quatermain series
Colonel Quaritch, VC (1889) Published in three volumes
Cleopatra (1889)
Beatrice (1890)
The World's Desire (1890) Co-written with Andrew Lang
Eric Brighteyes (1891)
Nada the Lily (1892)
An Heroic Effort (1893)
Montezuma's Daughter (1893)
The People of the Mist (1894)
Heart of the World (1895)
Joan Haste (1895)
The Wizard (1896)
Doctor Therne (1898)
Swallow: A Tale of the Great Trek (1899)
Lysbeth (1901)
Pearl Maiden (1903)
Stella Fregelius: A Tale of Three Destinies (1903)
The Brethren (1904)
Ayesha: The Return of She (1905) Ayesha series
The Way of the Spirit (1906)
Benita (1906)
Fair Margaret (1907)
The Ghost Kings (1908)
The Yellow God (1908)
The Lady of Blossholme (1909)
Morning Star (1910)
Queen Sheba's Ring (1910)
Red Eve (1911)
The Mahatma and the Hare (1911)
Marie (1912) Allan Quatermain series
Child of Storm (1913) Allan Quatermain series
The Wanderer's Necklace (1914)

The Holy Flower (1915) Allan Quatermain series
The Ivory Child (1916) Allan Quatermain series
Finished (1917) Allan Quatermain series]
Love Eternal (1918)
Moon of Israel (1918)
When the World Shook (1919)
The Ancient Allan (1920) Allan Quatermain series
She and Allan (1921) Allan Quatermain series / Ayesha series
The Virgin of the Sun (1922)
Wisdom's Daughter (1923) Ayesha series
Heu-Heu (1924) Allan Quatermain series]
Queen of the Dawn (1925)
The Treasure of the Lake (1926) Allan Quatermain series
Allan and the Ice-Gods (1927) Allan Quatermain series
Mary of Marion Isle (1929)
Belshazzar (1930)

Short Story Collections
Allan's Wife and Other Tales (1889)
Black Heart and White Heart: A Zulu Idyll (1900)
Smith and the Pharaohs (1920)

Publications in Periodicals and Newspapers
A Zulu War-Dance (July 1877) The Gentleman's Magazine
A Visit to the Chief (September 1877) The Gentleman's Magazine
Hydrophobia (letter) (3 November 1885) The Times
The Land Question (letter) (28 April 1886) The Times
About Fiction (February 1887) The Contemporary Review
Mr Rider Haggard and His Critics (letter) (27 April 1887) The Times
Our Position in Cyprus (July 1887) The Contemporary Review
American Copyright (letter) (11 October 1887) The Times
On Going Back (November 1887) Longman's Magazine
Delagoa Bay (letter) (17 December 1887) The Times
South African Policy (letter) (27 December 1887) The Times
Suggested Prologue to a Dramatised Version of She (March 1888) Longman's Magazine
Mr. Meeson's Will (18 June 1888) The Illustrated London News
The Wreck of the Copeland (18 August 1888) The Illustrated London News
Cleopatra (3 December 1888) The Illustrated London News
Hydrophobia and Muzzling (letter) (25 October 1889) The Times
The Annals of Natal (23 November 1889) The Saturday Review
Mummy at St Mary/Woolnoth's (letter) (25 December 1889) The Times
Mummies (letter) (27 December 1889) The Times
The Fate of Swaziland (January 1890) The New Review
In Memoriam (17 May 1890) Thompson's Seasons
American Copyright (letter) (5 June 1890) The Times
Mr Herbert Ward and Mr Stanley (10 November 1890) The Times

The New Land and Tenure Bill (letter) (12 March 1906) The Times
Garden City Association (17 March 1906) The Times
Mr H. Rider Haggard on the Zulus (19 May 1906) The Illustrated London News
To Be Proof against British Bullets: A Zulu Incantation (19 May 1906) The Illustrated London News
Housing of the Working Classes (26 June 1906) The Times
Mr Rider Haggard on Small Holdings (4 July 1906) The Times
The Unemployed and Waste City Lands (letter) (19 July 1906) The Times
Mr Rider Haggard on the Transvaal Constitution (7 August 1906) The Times
Vanishing East Anglia (1 September 1906) The Saturday Review
The Land Grabbing at Plaistow (5 September 1906) The Times
The Land Tenure Bill (22 November 1906) The Times
Publishers and the Public (letter) (19 February 1907) The Times
The Careless Children (2 March 1907) The Saturday Review
The Government and the Land (letter) (29 April 1907) The Times
Chambers of Agriculture (2 May 1907) The Times
The Government and the Land (letter) (8 May 1907) The Times
Miss Jebb on Small Holdings (15 June 1907) Country Life
Rural Housing and Sanitation Association (27 June 1907) The Times
St Thomas Hospital Medical School (28 June 1907) The Times
The Land Question (4 July 1907) The Times
A Plea for the Sitting Tennant (letter) (12 August 1907) The Times
A Literary Coincidence (letter) (19 October 1907) The Spectator
Town Planning Conference (26 October 1907) The Times
Dr Barnardo's Homes (16 November 1907) The Times
The Proposed Agricultural Party (5 December 1907) The Times
Mr Rider Haggard and Small Holdings (10 January 1908) The Times
Mr Haggard and Children's Legislation (13 March 1908) The Times
The Drink Trade and Common Sense (letter) (2 April 1908) The Times
The Zulus: The Finest Savage Race in the World (June 1908) The Pall Mall Magazine
Sparrows (letter) (18 August 1908) The Times
Sparrows, Rats and Humanity (letter) (5 September 1908) The Times
The Letters of Queen Victoria (letter) (26 November 1908) The Times
The Romance of the World's Greatest Rivers (December 1908) Travel Magazine
Afforestation. Mr Rider Haggard's View (1 March 1909) The Times
The Late Sir Marshal Clarke (letter) (13 April 1909) The Times
Mr Rider Haggard on Agriculture (27 November 1909) The Times
Mr Rider Haggard on South Africa (11 March 1910) The Times
Why? (letter) (25 April 1910) The Times
Mr Rider Haggard on Irish Agriculture (23 May 1910) The Times
Why Not? (letter) (12 July 1910) The Times
Mr Rider Haggard on Agriculture (16 September 1910) The Times
Mr Rider Haggard on Vermin (8 November 1910) The Times
Danish High Schools (21 December 1910) The Times
Sugar Beet Growing in Norfolk (6 March 1911) The Times
Rural Denmark (letter) (22 March 1911) The Times
Rural Denmark (letter) (3 April 1911) The Times
The Copyright Bill (letter) (6 June 1911) The Times
Mr Rider Haggard on Poverty. The Burden of Civilization (15 July 1911) The Times

Mr Rider Haggard and the Public Records (28 July 1911) The Times
The Farmers' Burden (1 December 1911) The Times
Egyptian Date Farm. The Financial Aspect (11 October 1912) The Times
Umslopogaas and Makokel. Sir H. Rider Haggard on Zulu Types (letter) (16 August 1913) The Times
The Death of Mark Haggard (letter) (10 October 1914) The Times
On the Land. Old Problems and New Ways. The War—and After. (15 March 1915) The Times
Soldiers as Settlers. After-War Problem for the Empire (20 August 1915) The Times
Raids by Air. Zeppelins and Zeppelins (letter) (22 October 1915) The Times
Women's Work on the Land. A Palliative in Hard Times (letter) (29 November 1915) The Times
Women on the Land. Town Girls' Unfitness for Farm Work (letter) (9 December 1915) The Times
Soldiers as Settlers. Sir Rider Haggard's Oversea Mission (2 February 1916) The Times
Soldiers as Settlers (letter) (7 February 1916) The Times
Soldier Settlers. The Future of Rural England (letter) (10 February 1916) The Times
Farewell Luncheon to Sir Rider Haggard (March 1916) United Empire
Soldier Settlers for the Empire. Offer from Victoria (18 April 1916) The Times
Sir R Haggard's Tour. Land for Ex-Service Men (22 July 1916) The Times
Sir H. Rider Haggard's Mission. Land for Ex-Soldiers (1 August 1916) The Times
Land for Ex-Soldiers. Outline of Sir R. Haggard's Report   (12 August 1916) The Times
Empire Land Settlement Deputation to the Secretary of State for the Colonies and the President of the
Board of Agriculture (September 1916) United Empire
Empire Land Settlement by Sir Rider Haggard (December 1916) United Empire
A Journey through Zululand by Sir H Rider Haggard (December 1916) The Windsor Magazine
Mr Wilson's Note. British Publicity (28 December 1916) The Times
Home Produce (letter) (22 February 1917) The Times
The Milk Supply (letter) (11 April 1917) The Times
Corn Production Bill. A National Measure (letter) (13 June 1917) The Times
A Protest and a Plea. Farmers and Meat (letter) (9 October 1917) The Times
Pig-Breeding. A Subject for Municipal Enterprise (letter) (22 February 1918) The Times
The German Colonies. Interests of the Dominions (letter) (5 November 1918) The Times
Light—More Light! (letter) (19 November 1918) The Times
A Great American. Tributes to the Late Mr Roosevelt (letter) (8 January 1919) The Times
Shut the Door (letter) (10 March 1919) The Times
Population and Housing. Emigration v Birth Control (25 March 1919) The Times
The Ex-Kaiser (letter) (11 April 1919) The Times
Empire Birth-Rate. Sir Rider Haggard on Emigration (17 April 1919) The Times
Ex-Service Men Abroad. Warnings from California (letter) (10 May 1919) The Times
Edith Cavell (letter) (16 May 1919) The Times
The Ex-Kaiser. Uncertainties of Trial (letter) (8 July 1919) The Times
Race Suicide Peril. Western Civilization Threatened (11 October 1919) The Times
The British Cinema. Production of Reputable Films (letter) (5 November 1919) The Times
Horrors on the Film. Limits of Publicity (letter) (19 November 1919) The Times
The British Museum (letter) (24 January 1920) The Times
Air Exploration and Empire (letter) (7 February 1920) The Times
The Liberty League. A Campaign Against Bolshevism (letter) (3 March 1920) The Times
Bolshevist Peril. Counter-Propaganda (4 March 1920) The Times
The Empire's Vacant Lands. Settlers and the Food Supply (14 April 1920) The Times
Films and Happy Endings. The Tyranny of a Convention (letter)   (21 April 1921) The Times
Land and its Burdens. Evil of Grinding Taxation (letter) (8 August 1921) The Times

Boy Emigrants (letter) (31 March 1922) The Times
Migration and Morals. Declining Birther Rate (7 April 1922) The Times
Labour Party's Programme. Confiscation and Class Hatred (letter) (28 October 1922) The Times
Efficient Denmark. Keeping the People on the Land (7 December 1922) The Times
The Egyptian Find. Tombs of Eighteenth Dynasty Queens (letter) (19 December 1922) The Times
King Tutankhamen. Reburial in Great Pyramid (letter) (13 February 1923) The Times
The Norfolk Dispute. A Truce while There is Time (letter) (3 April 1923) The Times
Rural Post and Telephone. Minister's Reply to Deputation (19 April 1923) The Times
Liberalism and Land Reform (letter) (1 May 1923) The Times
Small Holdings. Influence of Heredity (letter) (4 July 1923) The Times
Agricultural Parcel Post (26 July 1923) The Times
Country Houses for Sale. Empty East Anglian Mansions (letter) (14 June 1924) The Times
Plight of Agriculture (24 July 1924) The Times
Loans From the British Museum (letter) (30 July 1924) The Times
Zinovieff Letter. Mr MacDonald and a Political Plot (letter) (29 October 1924) The Times
Two Centuries of Publishing. Tributes to Messrs. Longmans (6 November 1924) The Times
Imagination and War (26 November 1924) The Times

Non-Fiction
Cetywayo and His White Neighbours (1882)
A Farmer's Year (1899)
The Last Boer War (1899)
A Winter Pilgrimage (1901)
Rural England (1902)
A Gardener's Year (1905)
The Poor and the Land (1905)
Regeneration (1910)
Rural Denmark (1911)
The Days of My Life (1926)

Film Adaptations

King Solomon's Mines
This novel has been adapted at least six times. The first version, King Solomon's Mines, directed by
Robert Stevenson, premiered in 1937. The best known version premiered in 1950: King Solomon's
Mines, directed by Compton Bennett and Andrew Marton, was followed in 1959 by a sequel, Watusi. In
1979 a low-budget version directed by Alvin Rakoff, King Solomon's Treasure, combined both King
Solomon's Mines and Allan Quatermain in one story. The 1985 film King Solomon's Mines was a tongue-
in-cheek parody of the story, with a 1987 sequel in the same vein, Allan Quatermain and the Lost City of
Gold. Around the same time an Australian animated TV film came out, King Solomon's Mines. In 2008 a
direct-to-video adaptation, Allan Quatermain and the Temple of Skulls, was released.

She
She has been adapted for the cinema at least ten times, and was one of the earliest films to be made, in
1899 as La Colonne de feu (The Pillar of Fire), by Georges Méliès. A 1911 version starred Marguerite
Snow, a British-produced version appeared in 1916, and in 1917 Valeska Suratt appeared in a production

for Fox which is lost. In 1925 a silent film of She, starring Betty Blythe, was produced with the active participation of Rider Haggard, who wrote the intertitles. This film combines elements from all the books in the series.

A decade later another cinematic version of the novels was released, featuring Helen Gahagan, Randolph Scott and Nigel Bruce. Unlike the book and the other films, this 1935 version was set in the Arctic, rather than Africa, and depicts the ancient civilisation of the story in an Art Deco style, with music by Max Steiner.

The 1965 film She was produced by Hammer Film Productions; it starred Ursula Andress as Ayesha and John Richardson as her reincarnated love, with Peter Cushing and Bernard Cribbins as other members of the expedition.

In 2001 another adaption was released direct-to-video with Ian Duncan as Leo Vincey, Ophélie Winter as Ayesha and Marie Bäumer as Roxane.

Dawn
The film Dawn was released in 1917, starring Hubert Carter and Annie Esmond.

Jess
This book was filmed in 1912, featuring Marguerite Snow, Florence La Badie and James Cruze, in 1914 with Constance Crawley and Arthur Maude, and in 1917 as Heart and Soul, starring Theda Bara in the title role.

Beatrice
The book was adapted into a 1921 Italian silent drama film called The Stronger Passion, directed by Herbert Brenon and starring Marie Doro and Sandro Salvini.

Swallow
The novel was adapted into a 1922 South African film.

Stella Fregelius
The book was adapted into a 1921 British film, Stella.

Moon of Israel
This novel was the basis of a script by Ladislaus Vajda, for film-director Michael Curtiz in his 1924 Austrian epic known as Die Sklavenkönigin (Queen of the Slaves).